NORA
GOES
OFF
SCRIPT

NORA
GOES
OFF
SCRIPT

Annabel Monaghan

G. P. PUTNAM'S SONS
New York

PUTNAM
— EST. 1838 —

G. P. PUTNAM'S SONS
Publishers Since 1838
An imprint of Penguin Random House LLC
penguinrandomhouse.com

Library of Congress Cataloging-in-Publication Data

Names: Monaghan, Annabel, author.
Title: Nora goes off script / Annabel Monaghan.
Description: New York: G. P. Putnam's Sons, 2022.
Identifiers: LCCN 2022006908 (print) | LCCN 2022006909 (ebook) |
ISBN 9780593420034 (hardcover) | ISBN 9780593420041 (ebook)
Subjects: LCGFT: Romance fiction.
Classification: LCC PS3613.O52268 N67 2022 (print) |
LCC PS3613.O52268 (ebook) | DDC 813/.6—dc23/eng/20220216
LC record available at https://lccn.loc.gov/2022006908
LC ebook record available at https://lccn.loc.gov/2022006909
p.   cm.

International edition ISBN: 9780593542064

Printed in the United States of America
1st Printing

Book design by Ashley Tucker

This is a work of fiction. Names, characters, places, and
incidents either are the product of the author's imagination or are
used fictitiously, and any resemblance to actual persons, living or dead,
businesses, companies, events, or locales is entirely coincidental.

For Tom

NORA
GOES
OFF
SCRIPT

CHAPTER 1

H OLLYWOOD'S COMING TODAY.
I'm not going to lose my house.
Those two thoughts surface in the same moment
as the sun starts to brighten my room. I've been paid for my
screenplay, and the bonus money for letting them film here
will hit my bank account at noon. Good-bye unpaid real estate taxes. Good-bye credit card debt. And to think, Ben's
saying good-bye to me has made it all possible. I don't know
how this day could get any better. I hop out of bed, grab my
heaviest morning sweater, and head downstairs. I pour my
coffee and go out to the porch to watch the sunrise.

Whoever buys this house from me, I always think, will
tear it down. It's over a hundred years old; everything's broken. There's a certain point in January when the wind blows
right into the kitchen and we have to duct-tape a fleece blanket over the doorframe. The floorboards droop; there are only

two bathrooms and they're both upstairs. Each bedroom has a closet designed to house six outfits, preferably for very small people. Ben had a list of house complaints he used to like to run through daily, and I could never shake the feeling that he was really complaining about me.

This house is a disaster, sure. But I fell in love with it when I first looked down the long windy path of the driveway. The magnolia trees that line either side touch in the middle, so that now, in April, you drive through a tunnel of pink flowers. When you emerge onto the main road it feels like you've been transported from one world to another, like a bride leaving the church. It feels like a treat going out for milk, and it feels like a treat coming home.

The house was built by a British doctor named George Faircloth who lived in Manhattan and came upstate to Laurel Ridge in the summer, which explains the complete lack of winterization. It was built to be enjoyed on a seventy-eight-degree day and primarily from the outside. I imagine his landscaping this property like a maestro, arranging the magnolias and the forsythia beneath them to announce the beginning of spring. After a long gray winter, these first pink and yellow blooms shout, "Something's happening!" By May they'll have gone green with the rest of the yard, a quiet before the peonies and hydrangea bloom.

I knew I'd do anything to live here when I saw the tea house in the back. It's a one-room structure the doctor had commissioned to honor the ritual of formal tea. Where the main house is flimsy white clapboard with peeling black shutters, the tea house is made of gray stone with a slate roof. It has a small working fireplace and oak-paneled walls. It's as if Dr. Faircloth reached over the pond and plucked it out of the English countryside. I distinctly remember hearing Ben use the word "shed" when we walked into it, and I ignored him the way you do when you're trying to stay married.

The first morning we woke up here, I got up at first light because we didn't have any curtains yet. I took my coffee to the front porch, and the sunrise was the surprise of my life. I'd never seen the house at six A.M. I didn't even know we were facing east. It was like a gift with purchase, a reward for loving this broken place.

I stand on the porch now, taking it in before the movie crew arrives. Pink ribbons, then orange creep up behind the wide-armed oak tree at the end of my lawn. The sun rises behind it differently every day. Some days it's a solid bar of sherbet that rolls up like movie credits and fills the sky. Some days the light dapples through the leaves in a muted gray. The oak won't have leaves for a few weeks, just tiny yellow and white blooms pollinating one another and promising a lawn full of acorns. My lawn is its best self in April, particularly in the morning when it's dew-kissed and catching the light. I don't know the science behind all of it, but I know the rhythm of this property like I know my own body. The sun will rise here every single day.

BY THE TIME I've gotten my kids up and fed and off to school, I've changed my clothes six times. I stand in front of the mirror in the same jeans and T-shirt I started with, and realize the problem is my hair. The frizz isn't as bad as it's going to be in August, but it's still pretty intense. People in Hollywood have tamed hair, or if it's wild, it's been professionally disorganized. I dunk my head in my bathroom sink and then get to work blowing out my hair piece by piece, something I don't think I've done since my wedding day in my childhood bathroom with my bridesmaids crammed in behind me.

When my hair is straight, it's still only nine A.M. They're supposed to be here at ten, and I know that if I spend any more time in front of a mirror, I am going to overthink myself into a panic. I decide I look perfectly fine for a thirty-nine-year-old mother of two. And it's not like I'm auditioning for this movie; I wrote it. I decide to go into town and do some non-urgent errands. Maybe I'll get home after they've arrived so I can show up in an oh-hey-I-lost-track-of-time kind of way. I'll walk into the Hollywood version of my real-life drama in full swing, like it's some kind of sick surprise party.

I kill as much time as I can by dropping a pair of boots at the shoe repair and browsing the discount rack at the bookstore. I stop by the hardware store to chat with Mr. Mapleton about his hip surgery and to pick up the stack of crossword puzzles he saves me from his paper each week. By ten o'clock, I run out of things to do, so I know it's time to go home and see exactly what a movie crew looks like and what the consequences will be to my lawn.

I've misjudged, and they're late, so I'm back on the front porch watching their arrival. I grip the railing as the eighteen-wheelers barrel down my dirt driveway, dislodging the lowest magnolia blossoms and darkening the sky with startled birds.

For a second, my whole property looks like a Hitchcock movie.

I never saw this coming. I'm as surprised as anybody that *The Tea House* is being made into a real movie. The last movie I wrote was called *Kisses for Christmas*, an eighty-minute TV movie with well-timed breaks in the action to make room for the forty minutes of commercials. The one before that was *Hometown Hearts*, which is pretty much the same story, but it takes place in the fall. My superpower is methodically placing a man and woman in the same shiny town, populated by unusually happy people with maddeningly small problems. They bristle at first and then fall in love. It's all smiles until one of them leaves, but then comes back immediately after the commercial break. Every. Single. Time.

The Tea House is a departure from the formula and is definitely the best thing I've ever written. The first thing my agent, Jackie, said when she'd finished reading it was, "Are you okay?" I laughed because, sure, it did seem like I'd gone dark. The story runs deeper, with heavy doses of anguish and introspection, and for sure the guy doesn't come back at the end. In the months after Ben left, I sold two fun, light scripts to The Romance Channel, but then this darker thing sort of spilled out of me. I'd tried to keep my personal life to myself after Ben left, but I guess some stories just want to be told.

"I mean this is great," she started. "But this is like a big film, not for The Romance Channel. If it's okay with you, I'm going to pitch this to major studios."

"That's going to be a major waste of your time," I said, pulling crabgrass in my front yard. "No one wants to watch two hours of angst and abandonment. I swear I tried to perk it up at the end, but no matter how hard I tried, I just couldn't stomach him walking back through the door."

"Nora. It hasn't even been a year."

"I know. So I need to get back to what I do best. Do whatever you want with this thing; I think maybe I just needed to get it off my chest. Everything okay with your mom?"

"She's fine. Give me a couple of weeks on this. This script is a game changer."

As the first truck stops in front of my house, nine of its eighteen wheels on my grass, I realize that the game has indeed changed. I hold on to the porch railing for support as two more trucks start unloading cameras, lighting, furniture, people.

A pink-haired young woman with a clipboard and a smile approaches me. "Hey, you must be Nora. Don't freak out. Cuz I'd be totally freaking out. I'm Weezie, Leo's assistant."

"Hi. Not freaking out. I can replant the grass." I reach out to shake her free hand.

Another woman, closer to my age in a black jumpsuit, approaches. "I'm Meredith Cohen, executive producer."

"Nora Hamilton, homeowner," I manage, still hanging on to the porch railing. "And writer," I add, because I'm awkward.

"Listen," Meredith says. "We're a lot. Hell, just Leo's a lot these days. We're going to make a lot of noise and a big mess, and then we'll clean it all up and be out of your hair in two days. Three, tops."

"That's fine; it's what I expected. I've never seen a movie

shoot before, kind of exciting." A red pickup truck pulls completely onto the grass, towing a silver Airstream trailer. "What's that?"

Weezie turns and laughs. "Oh, here he is. Of course, that's Leo. We're all staying at the Breezeport Hilton; he doesn't stay at Hiltons." She rolls her eyes and smiles again, like it's mildly annoying but also adorable that this guy is wrecking my lawn.

"Leo Vance is going to sleep in that thing? In my front yard?"

"It can't be avoided. He's quirky. But he's got a bathroom in there and we have a honeywagon coming for everyone else. So don't worry about your house."

The Airstream door opens and out steps a forty-year-old, shoeless superstar. His jeans hang too low and his gray T-shirt is torn in two places. His hair needs a trim, and he's way too handsome to play Ben. But then again, Naomi Sanchez is playing me. He squints up at the sky as he gets his bearings, as if he's emerging from the dark after twenty-four hours. It's eleven A.M. and we're only a ninety-minute drive from New York City.

Leo Vance is the highest-paid leading man in Hollywood. I know this because I've been googling him for three days. He has homes in Manhattan, Bel Air, and Cap d'Antibes. He owns a share of an NBA franchise. No kids, never married. A Libra. He's originally from New Jersey and has a brother.

I've seen every one of Leo's movies, which isn't really a credit to him. I've seen a lot of movies. He's a good actor, and he's most famous for his smoldering stare. I have to say, it's a little over the top. In his first film, *Sycamore Nights,* he gave his co-star Aileen Bennett a series of white-hot smolders that got him named Sexiest Man Alive that year. I guess it became his signature move, so he kept it up film after film, even when it was entirely unnecessary. Like in *Battle for the Home Front,* he's telling his newly pregnant wife that he has to go away to war, and he's smoldering. Or in *Class Action,* he's giving a commencement speech at a military academy and smoldering all over everyone's parents and grandparents. And don't get me started on *African Rose.* A refugee center with a wild malaria outbreak is no place to smolder. Leo Vance seems prone to the inappropriate oozing of sex appeal.

When the smolder is turned off, he has an impressive range of smiles that are unique to each film. They range from timid to maniacal, and I've always admired the way he can keep each one consistent throughout an entire film. I'm curious to see what smile he'll invent for *The Tea House.* What smile would he imagine Ben having? I can't even remember the last time I saw Ben smile.

Leo Vance is walking toward my porch, and I brace myself for an introduction. Perfection on the screen, scruffy in real life. He is going to be transformed into a man with a lot of issues who ends up walking away from the woman he built a life with. Leave it to Ben to be maddening enough to make me finally write something worthwhile. I smile at the irony of Ben actually helping out after all.

Leo brushes past me on the porch like I'm not there, then stops and takes a step back. "You're missing a dimple," he says.

"The other one's inside," I say.

He nods and walks into my house like he owns the place. Not much of a meet cute.

MEETING THE DIRECTOR, Martin Cox, is as intimidating as I anticipated. Weezie's gone in after Leo, so he finds Meredith and me on the porch. "You must be Nora." He's not tall but he's big, and I can't decide if he's physically big or if it's his presence that takes up a lot of space.

I shake his hand and try not to say anything else. If I start talking, I'll tell him what I thought of the final scene in *Alabaster* and why I think he was robbed of an Oscar. I'll tell him that the lighting alone in *The Woman Beneath* was sublime. Mainly to avoid using the word "sublime," I keep my mouth shut.

"So, can we see it?" he asks. I lead Meredith and Martin behind my house to where the tea house sits at the entrance to the woods. There is no path to it, just lawn, so that a consequence of visiting the tea house is almost always wet shoes. I'd left the big oak door open, as is my habit, because with the door open, you can see straight through the steel windows on the back wall into the mouth of the forest. It gives me the feeling of endless possibility.

The tea house is a sacred space to me. The space in which I have been able to preserve myself by writing. And, unlike the main house, it is airtight against the elements. I imagine the Faircloths approaching the tea house as I do, anticipating a fire in the fireplace and a table laid with tea and treats. I imagine lovers meeting here for hushed conversation and first kisses. Ben had always wanted to use it for storage.

It may have come down to that, for all I know. My belief that the last thing the world needs is more storage versus Ben's belief that he needed a third motorcycle. Among the many consolations around his leaving are that he took most of his stuff with him, and he didn't ask for the kids.

The tea house plays prominently in the breakup of our marriage, which is what earned it the title role. Ben resented the time I spent out there; he resented the work I did. He resented the fact that I'd been paying our bills for the past ten years. Which made two of us, actually. The more competent I became at taking care of our family, the more he despised me. The more he despised me, the harder I worked to make things right. Me writing in the tea house was a mirror he didn't want to look into. That's how it goes in the movie. In real life, I don't know, maybe he left because he just wanted more storage. Ben wanted more of just about everything.

Now, as we approach, I hear Martin catch his breath. "It's otherworldly," he says. "The photo doesn't do it justice."

I smile and keep walking. "Well, it's certainly from another time. This is where I write."

It's warm for April, and the slate roof glistens in the sun from last night's rain. Two giant hydrangea bushes flank the door. They're getting their first leaves now, hopeful celery-colored things, but soon they'll be bursting with cerulean blue blooms the size of my head. "If you could have waited until July, you would have seen these in bloom," I say to no one, because Martin has already walked inside.

"This is absolutely perfect," he says, running his hands over the paneled walls. He pulls out a walkie-talkie. "I'm back in the tea house. Bring the linens for the daybed, I'm going to need three o'clock sunshine coming through the back window. And a mop. Make sure Leo and Naomi are in makeup."

Meredith gives me a little wink, presumably to make me feel better about the mop comment. I give her a shrug, what do I care? "Okay, so I'll get out of your way, let me know if you need anything."

I GO BACK into my house, relieved to find it empty. Outside every window, there is activity—a catering truck, a woman chasing Leo Vance with a spray bottle. From the largest trailer emerges Naomi Sanchez, somehow all legs in a frumpy housedress. I assume she's dressed up as how Martin imagined me. I first saw Naomi Sanchez in *Hustler's Revenge* when she was about twenty-five. There was a scene where she discovered she'd been double-crossed that was shot so tight that her whole face filled the screen. Where are her pores, I'd wondered. At thirty-two, she is still the most beautiful woman I've ever seen.

I text Kate: Leo Vance was in my house. Naomi Sanchez is exquisite.

Kate: Dying.

I'm having a hard time figuring out what I should be doing. I mean I'm inside my house which isn't a writing-working space. Inside my house is a mom-ing space. The kitchen is still a mess from breakfast, and it occurs to me that Leo Vance has seen my pancake spatter and has smelled my bacon grease. I'm mildly agitated that he's been in here as I start to clean. There will have to be boundaries of some sort. I don't want to walk in here tomorrow and find him smoldering at my dishwasher.

I call my sister, and her nanny, Leonora, answers. "She's out with her friends," she says. Penny and her husband, Rick, live in Manhattan and East Hampton and are frequently featured in *Town & Country* wearing the right things with the right people. This is the first time in my life I'm doing something cooler than Penny, so I leave a message. "Please tell her I called and that Naomi Sanchez and Leo Vance are in my driveway." Leonora squeals, and I am satisfied.

Once my kitchen is clean, I try to think of what I'd normally be doing. It's Wednesday, and on Wednesdays we eat meatloaf. Of course! I take a pound of ground turkey out of the freezer and place it on the counter. This doesn't take as long as I'd hoped.

I WATCH THROUGH the corner window in the sunroom. They're filming the scene where I tell Ben that it might help if we both had a steady paycheck. It was the day he lumped me in with all the other people who don't have the vision to believe in his dreams. I was a drone, a robot, a slave to convention. I'm pretty sure it was the last straw. I imagine my words coming out of Naomi's perfect mouth, and I start to

NORA GOES OFF SCRIPT

think maybe this film was cast all wrong. How is Leo Vance going to be able to be as dismissive as Ben was when he's looking at a woman like that? It seems like people as beautiful as the two of them might have been able to work things out. No man's going to walk away from Naomi Sanchez.

I've been watching the filming for an hour when I realize it's time to go get my kids. I open my garage to find three guys smoking in my driveway. They drop their cigarettes and extinguish them with their shoes and move to the side and wave me out, like I'm in some kind of valet-parking situation. I have no choice but to drive up onto my own grass to get around the trucks and onto the dirt portion of my driveway that takes me to the main road.

It feels good to put the chaos behind me and drive out into Laurel Ridge where nothing ever changes. Ben bought into this town because he was literally out of choices. He wanted a big life in the city—Penny's life, to be exact. But when that proved to be too expensive, he wanted a big house in a commutable suburb. That was impossible too. As I got more and more pregnant with Arthur and it became clear that our walk-up studio apartment would never contain us, we were in a race against the clock. We had twenty thousand dollars to put down on a three-hundred-thousand-dollar house, and a three-hundred-thousand-dollar house was a lot farther from the city than Ben had imagined.

Ben told his friends that we bought a teardown in the sticks as an investment. It's an up-and-coming town, he told them, which I always thought was funny because this town's motto should be: We Are Neither Up Nor Coming. It's a

town that agonizes over progress of any kind, secretly fantasizing that it was the model for Main Street at Disneyland.
There's an architectural review board and a planning com-
mission whose sole purpose is to keep people like Ben from
making Laurel Ridge less quaint.

We have six or seven shops that have been in Laurel Ridge
since the beginning of time. These shop owners enjoy a cult-
like loyalty from their patrons. Laurel Ridge is a place where
you'll always be able to buy a hammer from a guy you know
and a bowl of homemade ice cream scooped by a teenager. A
handful of other businesses pop up and collapse as people
come from Manhattan to sell us designer vitamins and per-
sonalized dog cookies. They rarely last a year.

At the end of town is Laurel Ridge Elementary. I park and
find my friends among a group of parents on the playground,
like this is just some normal day.

"OMG spill it," says Jenna. She's standing under the basketball hoop with Kate.

"What?" I say, trying to be casual. "Just hanging with
Leo and Naomi, whatever."

"Is he cute? Does he give you that look?" Kate asks.

"Yes and no. Absolutely cute and he's barely looked at me."

"So, the hair's a waste?" Jenna's referring to the fact that
I've blown out my hair.

"Yeah, that was a little overboard," I admit. "If you saw
Naomi Sanchez in person you'd understand why he wasn't so
focused on me."

"Hey, Nora." Molly Richter approaches us. "Looking
good, nice hair." Molly's that classic bitch you knew in

middle school who never snapped out of it. We have to be nice to her because she's head of the PTA and seems to have the authority to randomly assign volunteer positions. We steer clear of Molly Richter like people used to steer clear of the draft.

"I hear you're playing Hollywood this week," she goes on.

"I am." It's important when talking to Molly that you don't offer any additional information or ask any follow-up questions.

"Well, cute. Don't forget that *Oliver Twist* rehearsals are next Wednesday after school and you've signed up to watch the kids backstage."

"How could I forget? It's all Arthur talks about." And I've shown my hand. I should never have blown out my hair. Kate gasps, like I'm sinking into quicksand and she has no rope to throw me.

"Oh, is Arthur interested in a big part?" Molly doesn't give me a chance to respond. "That's great! Because I was going to name you play chairman, and if he's going to be so involved, you'll be there anyway. Perfect." She jots something down in her Columbo-style notebook as she turns on her heel and walks away.

Jenna is laughing. "You're so screwed."

"Yeah, I hate to say it, but you are," Kate says. "If you say no, not that she even gave you a chance, she'll make sure Arthur's a tree or a stone or something." Tryouts were today, so I'm hoping it's too late for Molly to wield her power and blackball my ten-year-old. Arthur is in the middle of another round of spring sports disasters, and this play is a lifeline.

"I know. And it's fine. If Arthur gets a part, I'll get people to help."

"No one wants to help," says Jenna.

"Then I'll do whatever it is. This is literally everything to Arthur. It's the first thing I've seen him excited about since Ben left."

I don't usually mention Ben. Not because it's too painful, but because I almost never think about him. I've created an awkward silence though, and it seems to work to my benefit.

"We'll help," they say.

"You guys are the best." The bell rings and dozens of children pour out of the school. Arthur runs over to us, dumps his backpack at my feet, and chases a bunch of kids to the jungle gym. I'm not sure what this means about how his audition went.

Bernadette, the eight-year-old boss of my family, barrels over to me and slams me with a hug. "Did he say anything about your hair?"

"He did not; I should have worn yours." I smooth my hands over Bernadette's brown curls. They seem straight out of *The Little Rascals*, like old-fashioned hair.

"Let's go," she commands. "They're leaving in three hours."

"They'll be back tomorrow," I say. Bernadette looks at me like I've lost my mind. "Okay, fine." I call to Arthur, and he drags his body across the blacktop.

"Seriously? It's only three-fifteen. Does weirdo need to get home to stare at the movie stars?" Arthur wiggles his fingers, failing to seem menacing.

NORA GOES OFF SCRIPT

"How was the audition?" I ask.

"I got it." Arthur gives me a half smile that tells me he doesn't want me to make a scene on the playground.

I pick up his backpack. "Let's get out of here before I do something embarrassing."

BERNADETTE IS OUT of her mind as we round the last curve of our driveway. Arthur is committed to trying to seem like he's too cool for the biggest stars in Hollywood. They'd be lucky to meet him, he seems to want us to think. He's got a major role in *Oliver Twist* after all. "Mom, she's so embarrassing. Everyone at recess and lunch was asking me about this movie. We're like freaks in town."

We pass the Airstream trailer and two eighteen-wheelers before we can even see our garage. A table with pastries and sandwiches blocks my way. I roll down the passenger window and indicate the garage. A young man in a red trucker hat happily agrees to move his operation onto my porch, but not before giving each of my kids a donut.

"This is epic," says Bernadette.

"It's a donut," says Arthur.

I close the garage door before we're even out of the car, happy to be back in my cocoon. Everything outside feels infested with noise and tires and people making decisions who are not me. When I get upstairs, I'll pull all of the curtains. There will be homework, dinner, *Wheel of Fortune,* bed. Their contract says they have to leave by six.

As we climb the stairs into the kitchen, Bernadette goes

into overdrive. "Did you meet Naomi? Is she as pretty as she was in *The Mariner's Wife*? Is Leo here yet? Is he tall or not? Frannie says he's short and stands on a box when they . . ." She stops when we get to the top of the stairs and see Leo sitting at our kitchen counter. She's probably out of breath anyway.

Leo stands slowly, rolling up to his full height of about six feet two inches. He gives Bernadette a stern look. "I am not short, young lady." Bernadette smiles and blushes and covers her face all in a single instant.

"Ha! There it is!" Leo motions to her with his beer. Which is my in-case-Kate-and-Mickey-stop-by beer, I notice.

"What?" Arthur asks, a little alarmed.

"The missing dimple. I've been looking all over the house for it. Your mom's missing dimple is right there on your sister's cheek." Bernadette can't stop smiling, and Arthur rolls his eyes.

I realize that I haven't moved since we came up from the garage. I'm frozen with a half a donut in my hand. "Yes, well done. That's where I keep it."

Leo goes back to his beer, and after a silence that seems to only be uncomfortable for me, I say, "So, I'm Nora. I'm the writer, and this is my house."

"Leo."

"I'm Bernadette, and this is Arthur."

"Cheers."

"Are you supposed to be in here?" asks Arthur.

"I filmed my bit for today, now they're doing a few scenes with Naomi alone. Dark stuff, this film."

"Well, yes. I was in a mood."

"She's in a better mood now," offers Bernadette.

"Yes. And we need to get started with homework," I say.

"I'll just be a little longer. My trailer is hot and I was working on this crossword." He indicates the crossword that I'd been saving for tonight. It's Wednesday, and that's my favorite crossword day, not too easy and not too hard. My kids know this and look at me in tandem, neither seeming like they could predict what comes next.

"Well, okay," I say. Lawn, beer, crossword. I'm keeping score.

I stand by the sink, donut in hand, watching the three of them. Leo working my puzzle. My kids pulling folders out of their backpacks, trying to act normal. Bernadette needs markers; Leo hands her some. She watches him as she colors. Arthur has a sheet of fractions he needs to do within a minute, so he pulls up the stopwatch on his phone. I watch this incongruous threesome, a scene out of I don't know what.

"So, what do you usually do now?" Leo breaks the silence.

"Oh, I start dinner." Grateful for the reminder, I begin to move around the kitchen. I ditch the donut, wipe the counter, open the fridge. The ground turkey has defrosted on the counter so I just need an egg. I place the turkey in a bowl and crack the egg into it.

"Dear God, what are you doing?" asks Leo. Where other people get his famous smolder, I get the scrunched-up look of disgust.

"It's meatloaf Wednesday," Bernadette tells him.

"That can't be right," he says, mesmerized.

I chop an onion and add it. I throw in some bread crumbs. Leo cannot take his eyes off my bowl. "That is truly the most disgusting thing I've ever seen." And then as I begin to mix it with my hands, "I stand corrected." My kids laugh.

Weezie comes looking for him at about five o'clock and doesn't seem too surprised to find him tipsy. "Come on, let's get you back into makeup. We need to reshoot a few things before dark."

Leo makes what I can only call the agony face, the face my kids make when I tell them we're having fish for dinner. "No. Please. Don't tell me there's more."

"Of course there's more. We have one, maybe two days left here before we wrap."

Leo clutches his beer. "But it's so depressing. You guys, your mom is so depressing. I just can't take it."

"She's actually fun," Arthur says. "And the rest of her movies are kinda dumb but with super-happy endings."

"He's right," I admit. "Dumb and happy. This was kind of a one-off, sorry."

He studies his empty beer bottle. "Can't he just come back? Like have an epiphany or something and come back?"

Arthur hides his face by pretending to review his fractions. Ben having an epiphany would be a salve to Arthur's open wound. "He's not coming back," I say.

CHAPTER 2

❧

I WAKE UP THE NEXT MORNING TO COMPLETE SILENCE. THE cars are gone; the trucks are empty. Leo is probably passed out in his trailer. I pour my coffee and go out to the porch to watch the sun finish rising. Leo's trailer is an eyesore, as are the muddy tracks it's left on my lawn, but it is not blocking my view. The sun is putting on a big show, turning the sky a bloody orange behind the outstretched arms of my oak tree. On windy mornings it looks like its widest branches are dancing the hula; today it looks like it's offering a hug. *It won't be long, Nora. Soon you'll be back in charge.*

I hear something move behind me, and I turn to see Leo wrapped in a duvet, asleep on my porch swing. His slightly too long dark hair covers one of his eyes, and he is breathtakingly handsome. A half-empty bottle of tequila (wait, my tequila!) sits on the ground. No glass in sight. I consider going for my phone. My friends would get a kick out of a photo.

Asleep he looks younger, almost vulnerable. He has the covers pulled up over his nose. He must have been freezing last night. I want to wake him to show him the sunrise before it's over. I want to show him something that's not depressing because I know what he's going to film today. It's the breakup scene. Trevor is leaving. He never loved Ruth after all.

I feel briefly guilty that I've subjected him to my sad story. It's not exactly my story the way it played out, but it's the essence of it. Ben and I were in love at some point and found ourselves with two great kids and a life that worked as long as I kept moving. And then he just decided, meh, this isn't for me. Like the way you stop taking milk in your coffee. And then you act like you always drank it black, like you don't remember that creamy taste that you used to say you loved.

I should probably feel sorry for Naomi. She's the one being left. I'm happy she won't have to scrunch up her pretty face in an ugly cry. Instead, she's going to have to be perfectly still when he says, "I'm sorry, this whole thing was a mistake. I need a bigger life." Hopefully the audience will recall that Ruth has given him everything he has and that he's added exactly zero value to the marriage. She'll play it back in her mind like I did to make sure she heard it right. I don't know how actresses do what they do, but she'll need to make us see the moment she realizes that "this whole thing" is her family.

Man, is Ben an asshole. I decide to leave Leo alone and let his film crew find him when they get here. I have two kids already.

· · ·

THEY WANT ME on the set. I have a text from Weezie. I'm unusually excited, as I've been cooped up hiding in my house all morning. I've washed and replaced everyone's sheets, and I've vacuumed every possible thing, including the dust out of my refrigerator fan. I even tried to outline the main plot points of a new TRC movie but found that my mind doesn't bend that way inside the house. "Nora, you're wanted on the set," I say out loud because I like the sound of it.

I check myself in my bedroom mirror. I'm in jeans, a navy blue T-shirt, and flip-flops. My hair is still nice from yesterday and partially brushed. I decide that this will do. I know from experience that if I try to spruce up a little with better clothes and makeup, I'll arrive at the tea house looking like it's prom night. I do better in a come-as-you-are situation.

I walk across the lawn enjoying the bliss of slightly wet feet. My subconscious is triggered, and I kind of want to write, in that same way I kind of want a snack when I watch the Food Network. Tomorrow they'll be gone and I can get back to it.

The door to the tea house is closed. I open it to find Leo lying facedown on the daybed, Naomi pacing, and a cameraman talking quietly with Martin. "Hi." I give a small wave as I squeeze in. "Weezie said you wanted me?"

Naomi stops and glares. "Are you the writer?"

"Yes. Nora," I say. She is so much prettier in person that it takes my breath away. I want to see her face without all that makeup and stare into her poreless skin. She radiates beauty even though she's obviously ready to attack me.

"Why?" She rips a page from her copy of the script and shoves it at me. "Why doesn't she do anything? He's leaving. Yeah, he's a bastard, but any normal woman would cry or something. I can't just sit here."

Leo sits up and runs his hands through his hair as if trying to focus. "She's right. This is an intense scene; she should scream and yell. At least beg a little."

There'd been no screaming and yelling when Ben stood right here and told me he was leaving. Not because the kids were asleep, not because I was scared to confront him. I wonder now at the chain of events that has led me to stand in my office with the two most famous celebrities in the country trying to explain my emotional response to abandonment. "Because he's not taking anything," I say. "He's taking nothing. He never really loved her anyway."

"What the fuck." Good thing Naomi's not my therapist.

"It's the classic self-correcting problem. If someone leaves you, it's because they didn't want to be with you. All you lost was someone who didn't want to be there anyway."

Leo laughs. "Jesus. You're not much of a romantic, are you?"

"I am not. At all. I believed in marriage at any cost until that moment. Then I just let go," I tell him. And to Naomi, "You're not a victim here. Or anywhere. That's what this whole movie's about." Everyone's silent until finally Naomi starts to cry, Martin hugs me, and Leo mutters, "Oh, for chrissake."

. . .

TO BE CLEAR, I didn't set out to write some big treatise on victimhood. I really just set out to write a TV romance for my standard fee of $25,000 so that I could pay my back real estate taxes and keep my name from being listed in the local paper. Again. It irritates me to think people believe I am suffering financially without Ben. As if. Having Ben off my credit card has been like a windfall. Last month my credit card bill was $795.34, mainly food and utilities. Having full control over that number is almost my favorite part of my new life. That and being able to spread out like a starfish in my own bed.

I digress.

The story opens in a cute college town that looks a lot like Amherst. I wrote the meet cute just as it happened. Interior: lecture hall. Handsome Jay Levinthal is whispering in my ear, and I laugh. Cut to Ben seeing this interaction. Class is over and I am waiting to talk to the professor. Ben approaches.

"I've never met you," he says. I remember this exactly, because it's a weird sentence structure. The idea was that the two of us had never met, yet the way he says it puts the focus on him. You never forget your first red flag.

"I bet you've never met lots of people," I say.

"No, I mostly know everyone." And as if to prove it, he adds, "I'm Ben Hamilton." He has a way of saying his name like it means something, like it's supposed to conjure up a set of images and expectations. Like if you said your name was Oprah Winfrey.

"Nora Larson," I say over my shoulder. It's my turn to talk to the professor.

Ben turned up in the library where I was studying, at the dining hall at dinner, at a bar that my friends and I went to every Friday night. He wasn't the type of guy I'd normally go out with. He was so obvious in his confidence, so annoyingly extroverted. His energy demanded attention, as if the people around him were all worshipping at the temple of Ben. It's hard to explain what it's like to have a person like this focus all of his attention on you. I don't know if it comes across right in the movie, but there's this moment where you adopt everyone else's belief system, and suddenly you're worshipping too. No one could believe my good fortune, dating and then marrying Ben Hamilton. Eventually, I couldn't believe it either.

It wasn't until we were making the invitation list for our wedding that I discovered Jay Levinthal was Ben's sworn enemy. Which pretty much explained everything.

LEO IS DRINKING amber liquid from one of my glasses on the porch swing when I pull into the driveway with my kids after school. Two of the eighteen-wheelers are gone so there's room to park in front of my house. Arthur walks straight past him without saying hello. Bernadette plops down next to him and offers her dimple.

"You smell like my dad." She means it as a compliment and has confirmed my suspicion that it's scotch in that glass. Ben's, I'm guessing. I nearly lost my mind when he spent eighty-six dollars on that stupid bottle. I was glad when he forgot to take it with him, but I'm maybe more glad to see Leo drinking it unceremoniously from a juice glass. Ben would be so pissed.

"Lucky me," he says, raising his glass in a toast. He doesn't strike me as particularly drunk, more as a person who stays mildly buzzed all day.

"I like this spot," he says.

"Me too. The sun rises here," Bernadette confides.

"Right here?"

"Yep."

"Wow."

"If you stay, you can see it tomorrow."

"Happens every day?"

"I think so." The two of them look out over the trees, and I have the odd sensation that I'm the third wheel here.

"So, is everything wrapping up back there?" I ask.

"I think. They're reviewing just to see if there's anything we need to reshoot. I'll be back in civilization by bedtime."

Trigger alert: That's the kind of thing Ben might have said. He'd belittle the life I'd chosen and worked so hard to build like it was less than. At the corner of arrogance and cluelessness, you find the worst kind of person. I suddenly can't wait to have this guy off my porch, out of my space, and away from my family.

"Well, enjoy that. Come on, Bernie, let's get going with the homework."

BY FIVE O'CLOCK I have a chicken roasting in the oven and a bottle of sauvignon blanc in the fridge. Per our contract, they have to be out of here by six or they have to pay me for a third day. All I need to do is say my gracious good-byes and watch them leave. It was fun to play Hollywood for two days, but now I know that two days maxes me out. We need to get back on track, three people operating as a well-oiled machine. I need to start writing something new. Arthur needs to start learning his lines. Bernadette needs to get the stars out of her eyes. Plus, the tires on my lawn are making me twitch.

I relax thinking about the simplicity of writing for TRC. I'll get back to that tomorrow. I'll write a low-stakes romance with the happiest possible ending, with dogs and adorable children, chance meetings and homemade desserts. And I'll do it at no personal cost. This last thing was just some kind of silent scream.

At five-thirty I go outside, as if my "thanks for comings" will remind them all to leave. My kids insist on coming with me. We walk hand in hand to the tea house and see two cameramen carrying lighting equipment away. "All wrapped up," one of them tells us.

Inside, Weezie is pulling the linens off the daybed. "Hey, guys, we'll be out of your hair shortly." She replaces them with my faded sunflower sheets, the ones that were inadequate for Hollywood, and just like that the tea house is mine again. The stone floor is too clean and the fire is raging too aggressively, but it's close enough.

We all make our way out front and say our good-byes. Naomi stops to give me a hug. "This film really wore me out. But I get it. And I hope other people do too. It's important what you wrote." Bernadette just about faints.

I look up at Naomi because for some reason she's changed into three-inch heels for the drive back to the city. "That feels really good to hear, thank you."

She changes her voice for my kids, higher and louder. "Bye, cuties!" They say good-bye in their most grown-up voices, in self-defense.

Martin thanks me. He wants to know if he can come back to the tea house for a press event. I say no, and he laughs. We're on even footing. Weezie's corralling everyone into their vehicles as Leo steps out of his trailer to give a wave. So freakin' rude, I think. He's been trespassing in my house and drinking my booze for two days, you'd think he could walk twenty feet and say good-bye.

Arthur and I give him a wave just as Bernadette is running over to give him a hug. Either the fact of it or the force of it takes Leo by surprise, and he hugs her back. They exchange a few words, and he touches her dimple. He climbs back into the trailer.

"What'd he say?" Arthur asks when she's made her way back to us.

"He wanted to know if the sun was coming up tomorrow. I told him I think so and that he smells like Uncle Rick now."

"That's gin," I tell her. And we go inside to listen to Hollywood drive away.

CHAPTER 3

L EO'S MISSING." WEEZIE'S CALL INTERRUPTS ME IN THE MIDDLE
of *Wheel of Fortune* and my glass of wine.

"Missing what?"

"I mean, we can't find him. Bruno pulled the trailer right in front of his building to drop him off, no small feat he tells me, and it was empty. They didn't stop for gas or anything on their way. I'm just, well I'm kind of freaking out."

"Well, he's not here. Is that what you're thinking?"

"I don't know. It's just that he's been kind of off these past few weeks, drinking too much and sort of disconnected unless he's on camera. I'm worried."

"Okay, well he's not in my house. I don't have enough space that I wouldn't notice a grown man hiding. Want me to check the tea house? It's really the only other shelter and it's raining out here."

With a sigh and an eye roll, I put on my coat and boots

and make my way out the back door to the tea house. Through the rain I can see that it's dark. The door is shut, so that it looks like a dead end rather than a beginning. As I get closer and wetter, I start to lose patience with this sad, spoiled man who has the balls to just disappear and make everyone worry.

I throw open the door, maybe too aggressively, and no one's there. I stare for a few seconds at the empty daybed, the perfect place for him to hide out and get a little extra attention he doesn't need.

My wine doesn't taste good anymore when I get back inside. I text Weezie and tell her he's not here. She reassures us both that if something had happened to him it would already be in the news, which is good. We're both feeling maternal, I can tell, and we agree to call each other if we have any news. I'm glad to be in the loop, though I don't know why I even care. It could be because he's the lead in the movie I wrote, but of course his meeting a tragic end would just increase ticket sales. I try to review his whole persona to see if there's something about him I like. He's entitled and rude and never says thank you. I settle on the fact that I like the way he talks to Bernadette. I like the way he notices things. A noticer is a person who can never be entirely self-absorbed, though he's pretty close.

I lock up and tell my kids to go to bed. They want me to read a chapter of *The Hunger Games*, which is too dark and too old for them, but I agree because I want to feel fierce. They fall asleep on either side of me, and I decide to let them sleep in my bed. I drift off with Katniss on my mind, relishing in having reclaimed my domain.

. . .

THE SUNRISE WAKES me up if I forget to pull the curtains. This is the primary reason why I never, ever pull my curtains. I creep out of bed so as not to wake my kids and head down to the kitchen to press the button on the coffee maker. The sun is rising, those people are gone, and today I'll write. I feel Bernadette's signature giddiness bubbling up in me.

I throw my morning sweater over my nightgown and take my coffee out onto the front porch. It's glorious. The sky is a brilliant pink. The rain has stopped and everything has a just-washed look to it, like green peppers that have just been misted in the produce section.

"Hi." I swing around at the sound of this greeting and spill half my coffee. Leo is sitting up on the porch swing, wrapped in his duvet, feet tucked under him.

"People are worried about you."

"I know. I'll call. But come sit for a sec before it's over."

I'm too stubborn to sit, so I turn back around to enjoy the rest of the sunrise before I'll have to dismantle this guy. When I face him again, he is giving me a soft smile, a younger unguarded smile of someone who is actually pleased. He says, "Your nightgown is see-through. You have nice legs."

I make a mad dash to the swing and hide my legs under myself. "You're a real piece of work," I say, accepting half of his duvet.

We sit in silence for a while watching the colors dissipate from the sky. I don't want to ask the questions that I know will suck me into his self-pity. And he doesn't seem that inter-ested in telling me why he spent the night on my porch in the rain.

After a while, I say, "You need to text Weezie."

"Fine." He grabs his phone and types a few words. "Happy?"

"I was, about five minutes ago. In fact, I was ecstatic about today. But then I find a squatter on my porch and I'm worried I might have to call the cops and have a bunch of cars on my lawn again."

"What were you going to do today?"

"Write."

"Another depressing love story where there's no love?"

"No."

Bernadette brings a glass of orange juice onto the porch, rubbing her eyes. "Did I miss it?"

"You did," Leo says, making room for her on the swing.

"Leo! What are you doing here? Did you sleep there?"

"I did. Wanted to make sure you weren't lying to me about the sunrise. And you weren't. It was spectacular." Bernadette beams at him as he gives her the last bit of his duvet.

"My mom makes pancakes. And bacon sometimes." She might as well hang a FOR SALE sign on me.

"Oh jeez. It's six forty-five. Is Arthur up?" I leave the two of them swinging on the porch and switch into morning mode. Once Arthur is in the bathroom, presumably making progress toward getting ready, I change into my running shorts and sneakers. Today is still a writing day, and I'm not going to get derailed by Leo Vance on my porch.

I come downstairs and find Leo and Bernadette sitting at

the counter in a comfortable silence. Leo eyes my legs again and smiles like we have an inside joke now. I make more coffee, mainly because I've spilled most of mine. I start frying bacon and scrambling eggs. I have three English muffins left, which would have been perfect if I didn't have a breakfast crasher. I decide to go without.

Arthur comes downstairs clean but with the look of sleep still on him. "Mom said you were here. Why?"

"He wanted to see if the sun really came up on our porch," says Bernadette. "Which it does," she adds with a conspiratorial smile to Leo.

"The sun comes up everywhere, dummy."

"Arthur," I say, overly sternly, like suddenly I'm pretending to be Mrs. Cleaver. I place the steaming breakfast plates in front of the three of them and hear myself say, "Refill?"

The kids shoot me a look. "Refill," in the form of a command, not a question, was something Ben used to bark over breakfast. He'd slide his mug toward me, sometimes looking up, and sometimes not. I'd reply, "Of course" as I poured, and someone who didn't live in our house might have thought I meant, "Of course I'd be happy to pour more coffee in your cup so you can drink it." Those who had been simmering in this pot for a while would hear the undertone: "Since I made the breakfast and I'm going to clean up all the dishes and you're really just going to sit there the entire day, of course I'll take it the rest of the way for you and fill up your coffee too, you lazy . . ."

"Sure," says Leo, who has probably never poured his own coffee, so he doesn't know this is a loaded topic.

"Did you get wet sleeping on the porch? Seems kind of fun but also soggy," says Bernadette.

"Half fun and half soggy. Plus there's a reason people sleep on mattresses instead of wood." Leo stretches his arms in the air like he's trying to work the kinks out, exposing two inches of his perfectly toned abs. I have to look away.

"Well, you'll be back at your house tonight, right?" asks Arthur.

"Sure." Leo's looking for something at the bottom of his mug. "It's an apartment. But it's not that much more comfortable there."

Okay, here comes the pity party for the guy who lives in a penthouse. I need to regain control of the morning. "Guys. Clear your plates and grab your backpacks. Bernie, you have art today so bring your portfolio thing." They get up and carry plates and find their stuff.

Bernadette gives Leo yet another hug. "Come back sometime for another sunrise. Or even a picnic. It's fun here, I swear." Honestly, we are going to have to redo the whole talk about stranger danger.

"Thanks," he says. "And the bacon's good too."

We're standing at the top of the steps to the garage, door open and backpacks on. Leo's not budging. "So, maybe Weezie can send a car for you?" I suggest.

"Right. I'll text her," he says, not reaching for his phone.

I DRIVE MY kids to school and return home through my tunnel of magnolia blooms. Leo's back on the porch swing, wrapped in his duvet. I park in the garage and gather my thoughts. After a series of deep breaths, I head upstairs into the kitchen. He's moved his plate to the sink, which is frankly more than I expected.

I normally stretch on the porch before I run, but I don't need to hear any of Leo's wisecracks, so I do it in the kitchen. By the time I walk onto the porch it feels like his ride should be pulling up any second. "So, safe trip back to the city," I say.

"You're leaving?"

"I'm going for a run."

"Wholesome." He lets his duvet fall a little. "It's warming up."

"Yes. Okay, good-bye. It was nice to meet you. Safe trip. Again." I'm walking down the porch steps, and I know he's watching me. I'm too self-conscious to start running, so I walk down the driveway until I'm sure I've disappeared into the magnolias.

Two miles out and two miles back. I return drenched in sweat and sparkling with endorphins. My porch swing is vacant. *My* porch swing, I think.

I'm more surprised than I should be to find Leo with his feet up at my kitchen table. He's doing my Thursday crossword now, and I notice he's making an impressive go of it. This annoys me, and I know that's petty.

"No ride?"

"They must be really busy," he says. I'm suspicious. "Where's the rest of the paper? I looked outside."

"I don't get a paper. My friend just saves the puzzles for

me." And as soon as I've said it, I'm embarrassed. And then my embarrassment makes me feel a little ashamed, which makes me angry, and I don't like any of these feelings. Leo Vance was paid fifteen million dollars to star in *The Tea House*. And I'm living on borrowed crossword puzzles.

"I'm going to go shower," I say, already heading upstairs. I grab my softest jeans and my favorite grubby sweatshirt and take them into the bathroom with me. I wash my blown-out hair and leave it wet so that I'll look like me again today.

"WHAT IF YOU let me stay for a week?" Apparently, Leo's ride isn't coming. He is following me on my way to the tea house, hot on my heels and kind of ruining my vibe. I have my laptop, my special candle, my two sharpened pencils, and a mug of tea. And I'm trying to ignore him.

"No."

"I won't bother you."

"Too late."

"You can write all day, maybe I'll take some walks. And I'll sit on the porch a lot and look at the trees. If you stay very still you can see them breathe and wave at each other."

I stop and turn to him. "Are you on LSD?"

"No. I just need to get out of the city. Let me stay here; you must have a spare room. I'll pay you a thousand dollars a day."

"I don't have a spare room. Go to a hotel."

"Then I might as well go back to my apartment in New York. It feels like a hotel. And I hate hotels."

He stops as we approach the open tea house door. "Wow."

"You just spent two days in here."

"I wasn't looking."

Determined to ignore him, I put my laptop down and line up my mug. I build the fire before sitting at the table, placing one pencil to the left of my laptop and tying my hair in a bun and securing it with the other. He stands staring at me.

"What's all this?"

"It's a ritual; I'm starting to write. Next comes the candle."

"Oh boy." He lays down on the daybed, arms folded behind his head. He's facing the steel windows on the back wall, looking out into the forest. The sun's at ten o'clock so the forest is getting a little light. Today the palette is a mix of white flowers and brand-new celery-green leaves. It's beautiful to the point of distraction, which is why I write with my back to it. "I really like it here," he says.

"You've said."

"Let me stay a week, that's seven thousand dollars, and you'll never see me again."

Seven thousand dollars would more than cover new gutters on my house. New gutters would cut back on the rot I've seen slowly encroach on my hundred-year-old windows. I might even be able to fix the leak I've been ignoring in the attic. There might be money left for a trip to Disney World this summer, a last-chance trip before I wake up with a couple of teenagers.

Alternatively, seven thousand dollars would take a bite out of next year's real estate taxes, giving me the luxury of not having to scramble.

"Have you ever felt like you're disappearing?" he asks. "Like you're sure one day you're going to wake up and find that the truest parts of yourself have been replaced by someone else's plans?" *Um, I just wrote a movie about it. I believe you read the script?*

How many times did I wake up next to Ben and wonder, *Where did I go?* His face would reflect either indifference or mild distaste, and I'd try to remember back when I was a person who deserved to be loved. I didn't know what Ben was looking at, but it wasn't me. I was gone.

Leo's face is wide open, and I can see he's made himself vulnerable. He's in some kind of a free fall that room service can't fix.

"Yes, I have. But how is staying here going to help? Isn't there a retreat or an ashram that would do a better job getting your feet on the ground? With better food? And professionals?"

"The sun comes up here, Nora." A normal person, or frankly my ten-year-old, would tell him that the sun comes up everywhere. *That's how the sun works, genius.* But I know exactly what he means. There is something about the way the sun comes up right here that seems to wash the whole world clean. It touches every single leaf as it rises, leaving me both grounded and inspired. It was here that I started to find my lost self again.

"Fine. Seven days. Six nights. Today is day one. You can stay out here."

"Out here?" He stretches and looks around. "That's perfect. Where will you write?"

"Maybe you could be somewhere else between ten and two on writing days?"

"Ten and two?"

"Yes. I have a loose schedule. The sunrise-and-coffee thing depends on the time of year of course, but then I get my kids to school by eight, run until nine, shower and clean up until ten. Write from ten to two. Nap until two forty-five, get my kids at three. Homework and dinner. *Wheel of Fortune* and wine. Bed."

"Well, that does sound pretty loose. Spend much time in the military?"

"Hey, it works." I'm well aware that I'm not going to get anything done today. Apparently, I have a houseguest, and it's already ten-thirty so the schedule is shot. I'm staring at a blank page and the blinking cursor of doom, and I know I'm not going to be able to throw myself into a new project with the Sexiest Man Alive dozing behind me.

I look up and he's staring at me. "Am I bothering you?" he asks, but doesn't seem sorry.

"No. Well, maybe. I can just tell it's not going to happen today." I close my laptop and gather my pencils and mug. "I'm going to cut my losses and run some errands. You can rest out here." There's weight to the way I've said "rest," and I hope he hasn't noticed. *Rest.* As if a single man who wears makeup and plays make-believe for a living really needs a rest.

"Can I tag along?" he asks.

"On my errands?" I must have made it sound more interesting than it is. "I'm just going to the grocery store."

"Sign me up," he says, swinging his feet onto the floor. "I'd like to see your grocery store."

He follows me into the kitchen, and I grab my bag and my car keys. I freeze at the top of the steps to the garage. There's a little bit of bacon grease on the sleeve of my sweatshirt, and I'm okay with that, but I don't want Leo Vance to see my filthy garage. I don't want Leo Vance to get into my dirty Subaru.

"You okay?" he asks. I turn and look at him and am hit with the full impact of who he is. He sparkles a little, and I wonder if he still has any makeup on from yesterday's shoot. Whatever it is he's looking for in the country can probably be found on the porch, but he will find no healing in my garage. "Let's go," he says and opens the door to the stairway. He's heading down ahead of me, and there's no turning back.

My garage is technically big enough for two small cars, but with the lawn mower, the wheelbarrow, my compost bin, and a big sack of fertilizer, you sort of have to walk sideways to get in. There's a sweet smell of decay with hints of mold and manure, and I can't get the garage door open fast enough.

"Earthy," Leo says and opens the passenger door. He sits down, and we both survey the state of my car. There's a layer of dust over the dashboard and two juice boxes by his feet.

"Arthur's just recently started sitting in the front seat," I say, as an explanation, as if he was going to think I'm the one chugging juice boxes as I drive. My cup-holder is sticky with something and filled with coins and gas receipts. I can't blame Arthur for that.

Leo kicks the juice boxes to the side and puts his window down as I pull out of the garage. The magnolia trees that line my driveway are particularly flirtatious this morning, exploding with giant blossoms. It's like their hormones are reacting to the presence of an actual man. I'm almost embarrassed for them.

"So, how far to the grocery store?" he asks. He's looking straight at me and waiting for a reply as I make my way down my driveway to the main road and struggle with the answer.

Of course, I should take Leo to the Whole Foods in Pheasant Landing. I've only been a few times, but it is gorgeous and shiny. It's the Leo of grocery stores. It's fifteen minutes away, and we'd have to get on the highway, but it seems more his speed than where I shop. I'm having a hard time picturing him in the Stop n' Save. It's closer and much cheaper, but it's pretty shabby, inside and out. On the plus side, it has the self-scanners so I can effectively get through the store without speaking to another human being, and on Fridays it almost always has canned goods on sale. I am at the end of my driveway: Left to the Stop n' Save or right to the highway? I am seven thousand dollars richer than I was when I woke up this morning, so I could turn right if I wanted to. But I can't handle another guy forcing me to run up my credit card bill, so I turn left.

I PULL MY station wagon into the Stop n' Save parking lot and kill the engine. "Do you have any idea what you're getting yourself into?"

"I do not. That's why I'm here." He gives me a youthful, expectant smile.

"*Midnight in Jakarta*," I say. He looks at me, puzzled. "The smile. It's the one you gave your parents, the shopkeepers, even the chief of police in *Midnight in Jakarta*."

"That's creepy," he says.

"That you recycle old movie smiles? I agree."

"That you notice." He laughs and gets out of the car.

"Can you just try to fit in?" I ask, gathering my shopping bags from the back seat. He's in jeans and a white T-shirt and a black leather jacket that probably cost what my car's worth. "Maybe lose the jacket?"

He takes it off and suddenly he's all shoulders and abs and I have to look away from the excess of it. "Put the jacket back on," I tell him.

He wants to know what the bags are for, and I just shake my head. I scan my Stop n' Save card to use the self-checkout gun, and his mind is blown. "So, it just knows what you're buying?" He's turning the gun in his hands, peering into the reader as if he'll be able to see the tiny men who are making it work.

"Yes, from the barcodes."

"What about fruit?"

"I'll show you," I say.

An older woman who I don't know is blocking the entrance to the produce section. She is a statue with her hands on her full shopping cart, mouth open. Leo says, "Hello."

She says, "Leo Vance."

"Yes," he says.

"Leo Vance," she says again, not moving an inch.

"You've got me." When he's given her more than enough time to speak, he goes on. "Okay then, we have some shopping to do. I've got the scanner." He waves it at her and gives her a smile I can't quite name, but I've seen it before on the big screen.

As always, I approach the produce section with caution. Some shit's always going down in the produce section—women over-confiding about their marriages, odd confessions, inappropriate confrontations. Don't get me started. So when I look up and see Anita Wallingford coming my way, I'm not surprised.

Leo has his back to us, auditing the banana selection. He's mumbling about how cheap bananas are, even the organic ones, as he weighs them and prints out the label. Anita starts right in. "Hey, Nora! How're you doing?" Pouty face. "I heard about you and Ben. Just awful." I nod in agreement, hoping we can move on. "I can't believe you didn't call me. I mean I had to hear it from someone else, and I just felt so hurt."

This is a stunner, even coming from Anita. Even in the produce section. I can only repeat the words that have registered. "You're hurt because Ben left me?"

"You should have called me. I mean, I thought we were . . ." I feel a hand on my shoulder. Leo has turned around to meet her gaze.

"She's been super busy. I'm Leo." He extends his hand with what I assume is a smolder. I want to see it since he's never smoldered me, except I can't take my eyes off wretched Anita Wallingford. She looks at him and then at me, and then

45

at him again. The tiny microcomputer behind her eyes is overheating. She might short-circuit. For a brief moment, I love the produce section.

"Good to see you," I say, grabbing Leo's arm and walking toward the deli.

"What's wrong with that woman? And who's Ben?"

"Ben's Trevor. And I don't talk about him in the super-market."

"So it's a true story?" he asks. "You're Ruth?"

"It's mostly true, and I'm mostly Ruth."

"Badass," Leo says, nodding his approval.

I'm studying the chicken options. A whole chicken is $3.99 a pound, a whole chicken cut up is $4.25 a pound, and boneless breasts are $3.75 a pound. I swear sometimes the poultry section at the Stop n' Save feels like the New York Stock Exchange, where prices move randomly and only the most savvy come out on top. I confess that I am a genius at buying chicken.

"Did you have a stroke or something?" Leo is watching me watch the chicken.

"No, just calculating. I think we'll take these, so we're not paying for the bones." I grab two packages of boneless breasts.

Leo grabs a package of ground turkey. "Do you need this for your gross meatloaf?"

"Not on a Friday. Ground turkey goes on sale on Sundays. Almost always."

"Huh," he says. "When do we buy steaks?"

"Around Christmas."

.   .   .

LEO DOESN'T SEEM to have a lot of experience with bringing groceries in from the car, but he manages to fake it and carry a few bags up the porch stairs. There's a black Louis Vuitton rolling suitcase by the front door, along with a large white paper bag.

"What's all this?"

"Oh, I had Weezie send me some stuff from my place. And she picked up lunch from Louise's. You like lobster bisque?"

"I don't usually eat lunch. Why don't I get this stuff put away and maybe you can go eat in the tea house?"

"Sick of me already?"

"A little," I say. He gives me a playful salute and lugs his stuff out the back door.

I text Kate. I text Penny. I eventually receive a satisfying amount of shock and awe. Leo Vance is staying the week.

CHAPTER 4

⁓

I KNOW EVERYONE KNOWS ABOUT LEO THE SECOND I GET out of my car. Moms in lipstick and brushed hair greet me with disappointment. Kate's the first to ask, "Where the heck is he? And I didn't tell anybody, just so you know."

"We saw Anita Wallingford at the Stop n' Save, so that news is on the fast track. In a fun twist, she's super hurt because Ben left me."

"That sounds about right. Wait 'we'?" We make our way onto the playground, a safe distance from where the doors will soon open and our kids will spill out.

"Yeah, he wanted to come with me. If I hadn't snuck out, he'd probably be here too. I think he's having some kind of a crisis where he wants to pretend to be a regular person for a while. The price of bananas really rocked his world."

"They are oddly cheap."

"They are."

"So, where is he?"

"He's in the tea house. He brought his lunch in there—lobster bisque delivered from Manhattan no less—and that was two and a half hours ago."

"I just can't freakin' believe it," she says for the hundredth time. Our boys come out first, drop their backpacks at our feet, and run to the basketball court. Bernadette and Cooper, Kate's younger son, come out a few minutes later and head straight to us.

"Is it true that Leo Vance spent the night on your porch?" Cooper wants to know.

"It is."

"See?" Bernadette makes a face at him.

"And he's going to stay for another week." I hear myself say it and for the first time realize that my kids might be uncomfortable with this. Having him around might amplify their feelings about Ben leaving. And jeez, how do I even know he's not a pervert? "If that's okay with you guys," I add.

Bernadette jumps into my arms. "Oh, Mommy, this is going to be the awesomest week ever. A sleepover with a movie star." Once the hug is spent, she turns to Cooper, makes a face, and declares that we need to get home.

When we're all in the car, I try to explain. Yes, he has another place to live. No, he's not having a nervous breakdown. Maybe he just wants a little quiet and privacy. Maybe he wants to try meatloaf. Bernadette punctuates each of my sentences with an "ohmigod." Arthur is silent. He's silent as we pull into the garage, and as he starts unloading his backpack in the kitchen.

I bite. "Honey, is this okay with you? Are you upset I told Leo he could stay?"

"It's just weird, Mom. He's not even . . . Forget it. It's fine."

"It might be kind of fun," I say. "And it's just a week."

"It's fine." This is all I'm going to get out of Arthur.

Around five o'clock Leo knocks on the sunroom door. Bernadette races over to invite him in. "Hi! What have you been doing out there?" she wants to know.

"I ate some soup and read a little and fell asleep. Perfect afternoon. Am I invited for dinner? I was thinking about trying your weird food." He makes a face and Bernadette gives it right back to him.

"Dinner's included," I say. It's Friday, pasta night.

Arthur looks up from his papers. "Hey," Leo says. I'll give him this: He can read a room. He knows to come in hot with Bernadette but not with Arthur. He grabs a glass and my cheap sauvignon blanc from the refrigerator and sits on a barstool two over from Arthur. "Homework?" he asks.

Arthur barely looks up. "No, it's a play."

Leo asks, "One you're reading or one you're performing in?"

"I'm in the fifth-grade play, *Oliver Twist*. I'm Fagin. I only have five days to learn all this." Arthur holds up his script to illustrate just how much material that is.

Leo looks down at his glass. "Don't do it, dude."

"The play?" Arthur asks.

"Any acting at all." Leo looks straight at Arthur. "If you pretend for your job, eventually you'll stop being anything at all. A non-person. Silly Putty that you rub on a newspaper."

"Are you drunk?" Arthur asks, and I almost do a spit take. I am kind of wondering the same thing.

"Not yet," says Leo.

"Are you in love with Naomi Sanchez?" Bernadette wants to know.

"Bernie!" I scold her. "That's none of our business."

Leo laughs. "She's beautiful. But between you and me, she's kinda mean."

"The beautiful ones always are," says Bernadette, which makes all of us laugh.

"What else do you want to know?" asks Leo, pouring himself a little more wine. "This is awful, by the way," he says to me.

Arthur shrugs and motions to Bernadette, who certainly has more questions. "Mom says you're not having a nervous breakdown."

"True?" he asks me.

"I'm not sure if it's true, but it's true that I said it." I start peeling carrots into the sink.

"No, I'm not," he says. "But my mom died, and it's made me think about a lot of things."

I put down the scraper. "I'm sorry," I say.

"You know what's worse? I really need to go to the bathroom. I've peed in the forest a couple of times, but I mean if I'm going to stay awhile . . ."

Oh, dear God. My kids and I look at one another, neither of them matching my panic. Leo needs a bathroom. "I'm sorry. I didn't even think of it," I start. My house doesn't have a bathroom on the ground floor. I can't have him walk-

NORA GOES OFF SCRIPT

ing into my bedroom to use mine in the middle of the night. "Bernadette, take Leo up and show him the hall bathroom. And you guys can just use mine while he's here."

I mentally hunt for better towels. I seem to remember someone giving us really nice towels as a wedding gift that were actually too nice for me to use. I look in the makeshift linen closet. I look in the laundry room. Ben must have taken them, towels that would pair nicely with his leased Audi, which was also perfectly out of step with our income level.

I find two slightly frayed towels that used to be white and are now grayish and leave them on the toilet before I go to bed. I get up at midnight and take a couple of Clorox wipes and some Windex to the obvious spots and leave a fresh bar of soap. Around one A.M., I switch my bath mat with his, because mine is slightly newer. Why am I acting like such a lunatic? Because, I say to myself, Leo Vance is going to be naked in there.

IT'S SATURDAY AND he's up for the sunrise. I hand him a cup of coffee and try to remember him ever using the words "thank you." We watch in silence, and when it's all the way up, he yawns and says he's going back to bed. Must be nice.

Saturdays at my house kind of feel like a riddle to be solved. I've got to get a wolf, a sheep, and a chicken across the river, and everyone must survive. Our variables are soccer, baseball, dance, and playdates. Participants must be fed and hydrated, with multiple costume changes that take place in the car.

When Ben was around, he grumbled about Saturdays. I suspect his crankiness was twofold: the fact that Saturdays weren't about him, and the fact that the hundreds of dollars we spent per season on the kids' activities took away from his ability to buy more stuff for himself. "Can't they just run around outside?" he'd ask, apparently forgetting that he was raised on a steady stream of tennis and golf lessons at a private club. This was one subject where I actually put my foot down. All the economizing with on-sale chicken and leaky gutters was so that my kids could have the chance to try things they might enjoy. This made Ben bananas.

He'd ask over breakfast, in front of the kids, which sports he had to do this time. Then he'd show up at the events, admittedly not at all interested, and go ballistic at the refs or the opposing team's parents. Apparently, he did care a little.

This, of course, applied more to Bernadette, who has a fighting chance of making a team that's not legally required to take her. Arthur, on the other hand, has two traits that weigh on his athletic future: He's remarkably uncoordinated and completely disinterested in sports. These are facts, not opinions. I have seen Arthur stop running down the court in the middle of a basketball game to wind his watch. The disgust on Ben's face every time Arthur walked off the court was impossible to ignore.

Saturdays without Ben are twice as challenging and twice as good. The three of us figure out the plan together over breakfast—how the food exchange will happen, when the change of uniforms and cleats will go down, which games I'll get to sit through and which I'll have to drop and run. At the end of every Saturday we order takeout and congratulate our-selves on a job well done.

We pull into the garage at about six o'clock. The kids put their equipment away in the mudroom, and I carry up the pizza. The house is dark and I can see the lights on in the tea house. I ask Arthur to go out and ask Leo if he's hungry.

"I'm not going out there," he says, pulling a slice from the box.

"I'll go." Bernadette is already out the sunroom door. She's back in barely a minute, and her spark is gone. "It's messy out there and he's asleep."

I wonder if this is a bender. Maybe he just wanted to stay here so no one would be monitoring him. Maybe he plans to spend a drunken week mourning his mom. It occurs to me, once again, what a luxury it is to be single and able to fall apart. Not to mention the luxury of being able to buy yourself a week's break.

At midnight, I wake to the sound of the toilet in the hall bathroom flushing. I hear him amble back down the stairs and out the sunroom door. I don't know when I'm ever going to get used to sleeping with the back door unlocked. At least I know he's alive.

ON SUNDAY, LEO is up for the sunrise again. For some reason being up early feels like erratic behavior for him. So I say so. "You're up awfully early for a guy who drinks all day."

"I do not drink all day."

"Then what are you doing out there?"

"I look at the fire. I read. I watch the woods in the back. I drink a little."

"Well, you're welcome to come into the house if that gets old."

"I'm fine," he says. "Here, this is it. This is the best part." We watch the purple turn to pink turn to orange, and the birds are backlit on the trees.

We both sigh a little when the show's over. "Want some eggs?" I ask.

"Nah," he says and goes back to bed.

SUNDAY AFTERNOON IS beautiful, and we have all the windows open in the sunroom, effectively making it feel like we're outside. The door to the tea house is open, but I can only see the empty table, not the daybed, where I assume Leo is staring at the ceiling.

I have a pot roast in the Crockpot, which makes me feel like Super Me. Not only was dinner made before my nine A.M. run, but my whole house smells like someone's cooking me dinner. I don't ordinarily use the Crockpot on a Sunday, but I know my time is not my own today. Arthur's first rehearsal is Wednesday after school, and today's the day this becomes my problem. Today's the day that all of his "I've got this, I'm fine" nonsense turns into a meltdown. He hasn't got this, he isn't fine.

I know from my own childhood that when you are ten years old, the stakes are high. You are teetering between childhood and tweendom and any single action can push you forever into the realm of the uncool. The kids around you are unconsciously planning to ditch you in middle school, so if you're not an alpha child you need to be prepared with a backup friend group. Being in the fifth grade is sort of like trying to disable a live bomb, and if you're Arthur, it's like doing it blindfolded.

Arthur and I sit on the couch in the sunroom, sharing a script to run the lines one more time before I make him do it by memory. He's nervous in the way you are when you are anticipating your own failure, and he's decided that this failure is my fault. If it's not one thing, it's your mother.

"You're the worst Oliver, Mom. I mean how am I going to do my lines when you read like a robot?"

Sigh. "Want Bernadette to do it?" Please, dear God.

"She's worse than you. Go on." We flip through a few more pages of his first scene and I'm pretty sure he's about to cry.

"How about we try the music?" I suggest. "Bernie, get the soundtrack and we'll try to sing along to Fagin's songs."

"Fine," Arthur says, though nothing is.

"Oh! I like this one," I say. I get up and start singing, "You can go but be back soon," adding arm movements and a little side-to-side sashay. My kids are laughing at me, which is fine because, for now, no one's crying.

When the song ends, Arthur says, "Do it again!"

From the sunroom door, I hear, "Good God, please don't." It's Leo, shoeless, letting himself in. "You just . . ." He's shaking his head at Arthur. "Dude, you're hosed."

"No kidding," Arthur says. And he and Bernadette both crack up.

"Hey, I'm not that bad," I say.

"Nora, you are exactly that bad. I think your Fagin's more depressing than your movie," Leo says, and now they're all laughing.

We follow Leo into the kitchen, where he's helping himself to another of Mickey's beers. "Smells good in here."

"It's a pot roast," says Bernadette. "It's better than her dancing." More laughs.

I'm entirely comfortable being the butt of the evening's jokes. At me or with me, this laughter has swept all of the tension out of the room. What if I could just serve dinner to the sound of people laughing? What if Arthur gets so relaxed that his brain actually lets some of these lines in? Being tonight's punch line is totally worth it.

We sit down to pot roast, carrots, rice, and salad. I open a bottle of chardonnay, which I know I'll have to share. Arthur asks Leo, "So, do you know Fagin? Like in the play?"

"I do," he says. "And I know it isn't whatever that was." He's indicating me with his fork, and it's all laughs again.

"Yeah, I had a feeling," says Arthur. "Do you think he's a villain? It's kind of confusing, because he's pretty nice to the boys."

"I think he's the best kind of villain," Leo says. "He's the kind of villain who does something horrible but who we still love. You can see his humanity, even though he's taking advantage of those boys. Characters like Fagin get to the core of what it means to be a human being—we are both light and dark." We are stunned. "What?" he asks. And we all start to laugh.

"Where'd that come from?" I ask.

"That was a lot of words," says Bernadette.

"Well, this is sort of my wheelhouse. *Oliver Twist* happens to be my favorite play. And I've played Fagin."

"Aw, come on," we're all saying in tandem. Bernadette throws her napkin on the table in disgust.

"I'm not going to help you. I will not lead you down the path to being an actor," he says to Arthur. "It's empty."

Arthur smiles. "Do you seriously think I could become an actor with this woman as my mother. I'm half her!" We all laugh, and time stops for a moment where I feel the warmth of this laughter and watch the dimming light leave these three faces in shadow—my children and the most famous actor in America.

Leo pours himself another glass of wine, and I protectively fill mine. I'm learning. He takes a sip and tilts back in his chair in the infuriating manner of teenagers. "If I agree to read lines with you, just tonight, will you promise me you will never become a professional actor?"

I like to play the odds, and I'm thinking this is a pretty safe promise to make. There's a one percent chance Arthur's going to want to be a professional actor and less of a chance Leo will even remember who he is by then.

Arthur considers Leo. "I won't promise that. But I do need help." This makes Bernadette and me smile, just the moxie of it.

"Looks like you got a full set of dimples with that one," Leo says. "How much time do we have?"

Arthur looks like he's going to hug him but thinks better of it. "Rehearsals start Wednesday."

"Let's do this in the living room. We need room to move around." And with that, they're all business. I go into the kitchen to wash the dishes. I am trying to remember the last time an adult took over one of my responsibilities. Ben would sometimes run out for toilet paper or pick up the kids from school. It occurs to me now how long I've been doing this all on my own.

CHAPTER 5

I T'S MONDAY AND LEO'S HOLDING ARTHUR'S COPY OF THE
Oliver Twist script while watching the sunrise. "Hey," he
says without turning his head.

I sit next to him on the porch swing, noting that he seems
to have figured out the coffee system in my house. "It's really
nice that you did that with Arthur last night."

"Don't tell him, but he's kind of a natural."

"I wouldn't dare."

We're silent as the sun moves through a dark orange finale.

"Writing today?" he asks.

"Gonna try. What are you going to do?"

"I was thinking about going into town."

Which is how I end up not writing and taking Leo Vance
on a walking tour of Laurel Ridge proper. The town is pretty
much one strip of shops, a small grocery at one end and a
bookstore at the other. Leo buys cheese and a baguette at the

grocery. And a jar of jam in a flavor he's never seen before. He asks if he can taste the salami and buys a pound of that. He buys berries and kiwis like a kid pulling candy off the shelf by the checkout counter.

"Planning a picnic?" I ask as we walk out, laden with bags.

"Nope. I just liked the looks of it. Let's go in there." He motions to an overpriced housewares store that has no chance of surviving the year in this town. In fact, I've never been inside, on principle.

Two saleswomen are chatting behind the counter and go silent when they see Leo. So silent, in fact, that it's awkward. "Hello?" he says.

The older one comes out from behind the counter. "Hello. I'm sorry. I was just so surprised to see you standing there. In my store." I admire her honesty.

Leo puts out his hand and says, absolutely unnecessarily, "I'm Leo. And this is Nora. I'm staying with her for a while." Both women look me up and down, probably trying to divine what sorcery I'm using to put myself in this situation. *He gets naked in the bathroom across the hall from where I sleep,* I want to tell them. Someone needs to know.

Leo looks around the store, fingering every coffee mug, every throw pillow, every set of salad tongs. "I'll take these," he says holding up a set of ivory sheets and evoking a gasp from the store owner. Then to me, "What do you sleep in? A king?"

"Queen," I say in a small voice because (1) it seems like a personal question, and (2) it's possible I was harboring a fantasy that these women thought he'd seen my bed.

He picks up a set of queen-size sheets and hands them to

the lady. "I bet your sheets are crap," he says to me. When I start to object, he puts up his hand to silence me. "Just let me." He stares me down until I nod in agreement. "What else? Do you like your coffee mugs?"

"I do."

"I do too." He wanders around collecting small items until he finds the towels. "We need new towels. Don't even start to argue." Which, okay. He chooses four sets of the most luxurious towels I've ever felt. They're a light aqua, a perfect match to the fading tile in the kids' bathroom. He hands them to the slightly panting lady.

By the time he's convinced me that my wine opener is "trash," he's got more stuff than we can carry. The ladies happily agree to deliver it all to my house.

"Well, my house feels like it's had it's *Pretty Woman* moment," I say as we head to the bookstore.

"I don't get to shop. There's a woman Weezie hired who chooses my clothes. Someone else picked out everything in my apartment. Same for the other houses."

"That's weird."

"It is. Like, it feels good to choose a towel color, decide which bananas look good."

"Is that what's at the heart of this suburban crisis you're having? You want to make choices?"

Leo doesn't answer, and I'm afraid I've pried. I also haven't said "thank you," and now it feels too late. We walk into the bookstore, and I introduce Leo to Stewart, the owner. He asks if he can take a photo with Leo for his Instagram account, and Leo is gracious.

Leo touches the spine of every book, and agrees to pose for selfies with three customers. He chooses a book on French provincial cooking (he doesn't cook) and a newly released Stephen King novel.

I have to admit I like walking through town with Leo. People I know greet us with surprise and curiosity. Both of these things are better than pity. Everyone knows Ben left me. And everyone knows he sort of used me up and tossed me aside. "She did everything for that man," they'd say, shaking their heads. Besides Mrs. Sanducci, who is recently widowed at eighty-six, I think I'm the only single woman in town. *Look at me having fun,* I want to say. *Look at me next to something glamorous.*

We stop at the hardware store to check in on Mr. Mapleton, and Leo buys a spray nozzle for my hose because he thinks they're fun. I argue that I use my thumb and get the same effect, and now Leo and Mr. Mapleton have ganged up on me. "This woman lives like the Unabomber," Leo says. "Have you been to her house?"

"That's her, just the basics. And she'll use and reuse something until it crumbles in her hands," Mr. Mapleton tells Leo.

"You should see her bath towels," Leo says and laughs.

"I can only imagine," says Mr. Mapleton. "But not the husband. That guy was in here all the time, buying a slightly newer version of something he already had. I used to tell my wife, 'That Ben's got everything but a job.'"

I've heard this a thousand times, but I laugh because it's true and also because I like how he's always been on my side.

"And he took it all with him," I say. "I like to think of Ben wandering around the globe with six sets of torque wrenches."

Leo adds the spray nozzle to his bag with the cheese, and we say good-bye. "Enjoy your stay," Mr. Mapleton says. "I'll have my eye on you."

"WHAT HAPPENS NOW?" I don't even know how many times he's asked me this today. Last time the answer was: I put the kids to bed. Before that it was: We watch *Wheel of Fortune.* Preceded by: We have dinner. Between school and dinner was two hours of Fagin training. I'm not entirely sure if Arthur did his homework.

I pour a glass of wine and head toward the sunroom.

"Can I come?" I also don't know how many times he's asked that today.

I grab a second glass.

My sunroom is only big enough for a small couch, an armchair, and a coffee table. There are two ferns at all times, one dying and one getting started, on a regular rotation of grief and replacement. It looks out over the lawn to the tea house, where I can see Leo has left the door open to welcome him back.

Leo sits on the couch, so I take the armchair. He's in a button-down shirt and shorts. He looks like he should be in the Hamptons or Malibu, any place but on my sagging beige couch. "Will you write tomorrow?" he asks.

"I think so; I need to start something new." I take a sip of my wine.

"Let's hope it's not a musical." He smiles an ironic smile. I've seen this smile before.

"*African Rose*," I say.

"Stop it," he says. "So, what's the inspiration for the next script?"

"It's not inspiration, it's more like math."

He sips his wine and leans back into the sofa cushions. "Explain."

"I write movies for The Romance Channel."

"No."

"Yes."

"Those two-hour movies that are mostly commercials?"

"Well, I've written a lot of them. That's what I do."

"Hilarious." He pours us each a little more wine, killing the bottle. "So why is it math?"

"Maybe not math. Did you ever play Mad Libs as a kid? Where you have to fill in the nouns, adjectives, and verbs, and then there's a story?"

"Yes."

"That's what I do."

"I don't understand."

"Give me a gender, a location, and a career."

"Okay . . . female, Chicago, real estate developer."

"Okay, easy. Stephanie, a young urban real estate developer, takes a trip to rural Illinois to look into buying a dairy farm and turning it into a corporate retreat center. The young handsome owner of the farm doesn't want to sell, and they butt heads. But as she spends more time on the farm, she sees

NORA GOES OFF SCRIPT

how important it is to the community and they fall in love. In fact, she's helping him organize the annual Founders' Day festival later next week. They kiss. The night before Founders' Day, she gets a call that she needs to shut down the farm immediately or lose her job. She leaves for Chicago. He is heartbroken."

"Oh no."

"Oh yes. But wait, now it's Founders' Day, and you can pretty much insert any community event here—Christmas tree lighting, soup kitchen opening, children's recital—and he's plugging along, and who comes back? Stephanie!"

"Yes!"

"She's gone back to Chicago and has realized big city living isn't for her. She's going to stay out in the sticks, and oh, P.S., she has a brilliant idea for how to save the farm. The end."

"That's so stupid. Is it always the same?"

I down the rest of my wine. "Pretty much. I change the names and the kind of farm, for good measure. And I flip the genders. Half the time the guy leaves."

"But he always comes back?"

"Always." A moment passes between us, where I'm pretty sure we're both thinking about Ben. For some reason I need Leo to know that I don't want Ben back, that I'm happy and whole with him gone.

He goes ahead and says it. "But Trevor left, end of story."

"Yep," I say. Leo's giving me this look, like maybe I'm a puzzle he's about to solve. "Well, now you know all my secrets. I'm going to bed."

CHAPTER 6

ᘓᕤᕤᘔ

L EO ISN'T UP FOR THE SUNRISE. I SHOULD BE GLAD TO
have the swing all to myself, but I'm not. This alarms
me on the deepest level. I'm getting used to him and
how he follows me around. I like how he listens to me when I
talk. I like how he looks at me.

Ben used to sit at the kitchen island and talk about real
estate and what's wrong with people while I made dinner.
"You know what's wrong with Mickey?" Or "You know
what's wrong with that guy at the bank?" These were rhetorical questions, and the only real variety to them was which
person had wronged him that day. He liked to keep the TV
on at all times, background noise while he moved the papers
outlining his newest scheme around on the kitchen table. Ben
took up a lot of space.

The night he told me he was leaving, he slept on the couch
with the TV blaring. I lay in bed trying to process what was

happening. The whole thing was so confusing. I remembered Penny's face the first time I told her I was seriously dating him. "Oh. My. God," she'd said. "Don't blow it." Ben was kind of a catch. He went to prep school and moved through life like a knife through soft butter. Ben was the kind of guy Penny would know.

Penny and I grew up in Chesterville, Connecticut, a medium-size town that had previously been two small towns—one affluent, one working class. When things were rezoned in the 1950s to create a single town with a single public high school, the result was a town divided like you'd see in a John Hughes movie. If you lived up the hill, your parents were likely professionals. If you lived down the hill, your parents worked a trade. If you were me, your dad was in the business of cleaning all the professionals' pools.

The divide in our town was something I almost never thought about. I took the bus to school with the kids in my neighborhood, and we played in one another's yards after school. We spent our vacations at the public pool, which my dad also cleaned. In high school, my friends and I made fun of the hilltoppers' pretentious clothes and sweet-sixteen convertibles that were invariably crashed and replaced within a month. I felt comfortable in my little house, in my faded jeans, where I knew exactly what to expect.

But not Penny. She wanted to be up that hill. Starting in middle school, she emulated the hilltop girls and the way they put themselves together. When they bought new skinny jeans, Penny spent the weekend on my mom's sewing machine tapering the legs of her Levi's. When they cut bangs, Penny followed suit. This never would have gotten her anywhere, but in the tenth grade Penny tried out for the spring musical and landed a leading role along with a handful of the hilltop girls. After prolonged exposure to Penny's giant heart and passion for fun, they became her real friends. The transition was seamless, making me think that Penny had always been a hilltopper just biding her time in our twelve-hundred-square-foot ranch.

Throughout college and when she moved to Manhattan afterward, these were the circles in which she ran. I was surprised to learn that these circles are everywhere and they overlap in the oddest ways. Rich people, it seems, all know one another tangentially. So I guess I wasn't surprised when I called her from Amherst to tell her about Ben, and she knew exactly who he was.

While I never bought into the glamour of the hilltopper, when I met Ben I sort of became taken by the ease of it all. His quiet expectation that the world would arrange itself around his whims. His confidence that he would never be called out or punished for any wrongdoing. He was that kind of slightly mean guy that made you feel superior if he liked you. Since the day he picked me, I'd done everything I could not to blow it. And yet here we were.

When we graduated, I had a job in publishing in Manhattan, and Ben had his first big idea and a check for ten thousand dollars from his grandmother. It would be six months before he learned this was the last check he'd be receiving. We found a walk-up apartment in the East Village that we could almost afford, and I think we were happy. I'd come home from work and find him at the kitchen table, excited about a potential new investor. I'd cook as he shared the real-time details of their conversation. I figured he was too excited about his day to ask about mine.

By the time we married at twenty-six, the glow had worn off. Ben was still railing against the injustice of having no passive income, an injustice that fueled his rage against the simplemindedness of the investors who weren't interested in his schemes. The part of me that knows who I am and knew I shouldn't marry Ben had become hard to hear over the din of wedding plans. Newton must have been thinking of twenty-somethings in long-term relationships with hard-to-secure wedding venues when he decided that objects in motion tend to stay in motion.

When I was two kids and one broken house into the marriage, I had to face the fact that Ben didn't really like much about me at all. He didn't like my worldview, my hair, my house. He was blind to my best qualities, and eventually I was too. I think our whole marriage was about me trying to make him glad he picked me. I humored him about his poorly thought-out projects. I made the money but did it quietly so he could feel like his work was what mattered, like I was waiting tables while he finished medical school. I even started using his words to describe my work, "another dumb romance." I cooked the food and tried to be upbeat for the kids. I remembered his mother's birthday and sent her gifts. It wasn't enough.

In my mind, I was holding Ben up; in his, I was holding him back. He had a way of making me feel like every time

NORA GOES OFF SCRIPT

another project fell apart, it was my fault. And there was no reason there, no logical connection, but the not-so-quiet implication was that it was me who was keeping him down. One night when I discovered we had thirty-seven dollars to our name, I suggested we eat at home rather than meeting friends out. "You have scarcity in your heart, Nora. You'll always be broke," he'd told me, disgusted. *I have a husband who doesn't work and tears through money like he's printing it,* I'd thought. *Yes. I'll always be broke.*

That night, alone in my bed with Ben on the couch, I fell asleep clinging to the oddest thoughts. Among them was that starting tomorrow I'd have full control of the TV. Starting tonight, I'd be going to bed without Ben next to me, pestering me for bad sex. I imagined tomorrow's sunrise and how that would be the last sunrise I'd ever watch with him in the house. The remaining sunrises would all be mine. I felt a profound relief that the struggle was over, like if you stopped treading water and then found yourself effortlessly floating to the surface. *Go, Ben. Go find your big life.*

Of course, it wasn't just me. Ben was walking out on his kids too. And that was going to hurt them for a long time. But in my new buoyancy, I couldn't help but think that I'd never again register the doubt on their faces as he promised them something we couldn't afford. I'd never again have to explain "what Daddy really meant when he said that mean thing." This was going to take some time for them to adjust to, but in my heart, I knew they were better off with him gone.

The next morning, I woke up thinking about Arthur's vocabulary test. He'd bombed the last one and was nervous to try again. I pictured him tackling all those tough words just after his father told him he was leaving. I ran downstairs and woke Ben. "Can we just wait until after school to tell the kids?"

"I'm leaving, Nora. You're just going to have to accept it. I'm sorry." He rubbed his eyes and turned back into the couch, and I thought, *Man, the disconnect is real.*

"I know, and I'll come to terms with it," I played along. "But let's just let the kids have their school day, and we can tell them in the afternoon."

"Sounds good," he said, sitting up and meeting my gaze. "I'm going to shower."

Over breakfast, Ben acted like everything was normal. I took the kids to school and went out to the tea house while he packed his things. I was anxious over the details of what was to come, but also a little nervous that he'd come out and tell me he'd changed his mind. I caught myself smiling out the tea house windows, wondering if maybe the future had actually just opened up. I never would have had the courage to let go of the rope in this tug-of-war, but Ben had done it for me.

When the kids were back from school, we sat them down and Ben told them he was leaving for a while. Arthur started to cry instantly, having the wisdom to know where this was headed. "Where are you going?" he asked.

"Asia," Ben said. As if that explained everything.

"I'll come with you," said Arthur. "I can help you there, and we'll learn Chinese." He spoke through tears and this is when my heart broke a little. I was better off without Ben, and my kids were too, but seeing the desperation behind Arthur's eyes killed me.

NORA GOES OFF SCRIPT

"Sorry, buddy, but I'll be back."

"When?" asked Bernadette.

"Soon." He gave them each a hug. "You guys be good for your mom, okay?"

They didn't reply, just looked at him in what I assume was disbelief. He grabbed his keys and his phone and his stupid puffer vest and left. We three stayed in the same room for the rest of the day, none of us wanting anyone out of our sight. For weeks afterward, I tried to get them to talk about it. Bernadette seemed more annoyed than hurt, like whatever her dad had to do that was dragging him away was probably nonsense. I was careful not to agree. Arthur was sad and asked a lot of questions I didn't have answers to. *Doesn't he miss us? Does he wonder how we are?* We talked about it every day for a while, until we'd sort of exhausted our own explanations. None of us thought he was coming back.

The house was bigger without his stuff and his anger. I cleared out furniture and luxuriated in the open spaces. I felt like the house could finally breathe. I started running before I wrote, and I swear my writing got better. I hoped my kids could feel how much stronger I was without Ben dragging me down. Without Ben, I had the energy to be mother and father and provider and playmate. People usually talk about their new normal as some sort of difficult adjustment, but mine left me lighter. I was released from worrying about what Ben would spend. I no longer needed to deflect his criticisms of the kids or myself. I was free.

But Leo in my house is fun. I like the space he takes up. It's light and exciting, and I am slipping into a daydream that this is my new reality. I have a handsome playmate who listens to me when I speak. He asks follow-up questions because he wants to hear more. I cannot shake the feeling that Leo likes talking to me. Like, he likes the actual me. He's not in it for the free meal or anything I can do to improve his situation. Leo Vance is just fine without me, yet he still follows me around with rapt attention.

He's leaving in two days, and I need to screw my head on straight. It's Tuesday. Bernadette has dance after school. I have to get the recycling out. Tomorrow is the first day of rehearsals and I'm in charge of shushing the children while they wait their turns. I'm also, as it turns out, in charge of the whole play, so I'd better get a committee together. Costumes? Sets? Snacks?

"Crap. I almost missed it." Leo barrels through the door with a blanket in his arms. He sits down next to me and covers us both up. The sun's halfway up and he hasn't missed the best of it. This is the part where the pink starts to move up the trees.

"Want me to get you some coffee?" I ask, because I'd never do this without coffee.

"No. Stay till it's over."

So I do and we sit there and stare in silence until the sky is bright. "What were you thinking about?" he asks. "You were all furrowed when I came out."

"Nothing." Talking about Ben is going to make me feel like a loser, so I'm quiet. Leo turns his head to me and gives me a look like he's not buying it. I say, "How nice it is that Ben's gone."

"Where is he now?"

"Who knows. He said Asia."

"So, you don't hear from him? He doesn't see the kids?"

"Nope. Well, he calls sometimes and makes plans but doesn't show."

"Wow. Where do the checks come from?"

And I laugh at this, a real whole-bodied laugh that ends in my coughing up a little of my coffee. Leo offers his blanket to wipe my mouth. I use my sleeve. "Sorry," I say, gathering myself. "That was a totally legitimate question. This part wasn't in the script. He doesn't send checks. Our deal was pretty cut and dried—I get the house, the mortgage, the credit card debt, and the pleasure of supporting the kids and myself. And he gets to walk away. I didn't argue because I didn't want to have to sell the house. And I actually might have ended up paying him alimony for the rest of his life. And then I'd probably have to kill him. So. This was for the best."

"I'm starting to see why Ruth was so nonplussed when Trevor left. So just like in the movie, he's sort of too good to work?"

"'Hamiltons don't work for other people.' That's sort of their thing. His great-grandfather actually worked hard and made a fortune in cattle. Ben grew up with that wealth but didn't really internalize the 'work hard' part of the story. It's like he missed the part where his great-grandfather shoveled cow shit for years before he made it. So he dabbles. He tries lots of stuff that doesn't work out, mainly because other people are incompetent." I hold his gaze to show him that I really am okay with it. Which I am. Not the part that he's made no effort to see or contact the kids in nearly a year, that part lives in my chest in the form of an easily triggered rage. But the part where Ben is who he is and it's not my problem anymore, that's fine with me.

Leo studies the tree line again and then looks back at me. "What happened to the see-through nightgown?"

"I learned my lesson," I say with a sisterly nudge.

CHAPTER 7

LEO WALKS INTO TOWN TO GET ANOTHER BAGUETTE from the grocery, so it's my chance to have the tea house to myself. It's mostly how I left it, with the exception of the much nicer sheets. His suitcase is open at the foot of the daybed, and I resist the urge to inspect its contents. The bed is unmade, and I imagine I can see the outline of him sleeping there. He'd be on his side with the line of his bare back mimicking the curve of the headboard. *Oh my God, Nora, stop it.*

I write from ten to two, and Leo mostly leaves me alone. I hear a car pull into the driveway and assume it's his lunch coming from some five-star restaurant in the city. At around one o'clock he knocks on the open tea house door. "Can I just come in for a nap?"

"Sure. No talking."

I hear him get under the covers and find a comfortable position. I stop typing because I can feel him watching me.

"What?" I ask without looking up.

"What's the gender, city, and profession this time?"

I smile at my laptop. "I'm pretty much working with what you gave me. A male real estate developer in Minneapolis goes out to buy a struggling pumpkin farm."

"Pumpkin farm? Is that even a thing?"

"Oh, you're going to have to come back here in October."

"Okay," he says, and I start typing again.

SINCE LEO'S IN my napping spot, I go back into the house around two o'clock. There's a case of French wine on the counter and a box of cupcakes from Cupcake Castle in SoHo. I get the chills just thinking about how excited my kids are going to be.

When I get back from picking up the kids, Leo is up and unpacking the case of wine. "We can't keep drinking that awful chardonnay. I hear this pairs perfectly with . . . What do we eat on Tuesdays?"

"Tacos," my kids say together.

"Ah, of course." He's laid out the cupcakes on a platter I didn't know I had and watches them disappear with satisfaction.

I am aware that this sparkly scene is a fantasy, but I let myself enjoy it. Smiling children and the promise of fine wine with a terrifyingly attractive man. Thursday's going to be brutal.

"Okay, so Bernadette has dance at four-thirty. Arthur, if you want to bring your script we can run some lines while we wait."

"Forbidden," says Leo. "You're not getting anywhere near that script."

"Duh," says Arthur. "I'll just stay here and work with Leo." He remembers himself and turns to Leo. "I mean, if you're not busy."

"Dude, if there's one thing I'm not, it's busy. There isn't even Wi-Fi back there." He leans over and messes Arthur's hair, and the late afternoon sun shines through the back windows as time pauses on their smiles, and I really need to get the hell out of here.

When Bernadette runs into the dance studio, I sit on the bench outside hoping I'll have a second to collect my thoughts. I'm horrified by how I lie in bed at night and wait for the sound of his feet walking up the stairs to the bathroom. I'm ashamed of how my whole system is on overdrive the second I wake up, how I've taken to washing my hair every day. My self-recrimination is interrupted by Sandra Wells and Kiki Lee, who usher their girls inside and take over the rest of the bench.

"Hey, Nora. How's it going?" starts Sandra.

"Oh, cut the crap," Kiki says. "Spill it."

"He's just staying for a few days. I think he thinks our simple life out here is a cure for his exciting life."

"Is he as hot in person?" Kiki wants to know. "Like does he look at you that way while you're buttering toast?"

"The smolder? No." I laugh. "That's just for the camera.

He looks at me like I'm some suburban mom who maybe needs a makeover." Even as I say this, I know it's not true. He looks at me with an amused curiosity most of the time. He watches me when he thinks I'm engrossed with something else. It's been nearly a week since I was actually engrossed with something else.

Bernadette and I enter the house to the sound of the two of them singing "You've Got to Pick a Pocket or Two," standing on opposite ends of the couch. Leo yells "Bravo!" and Arthur bows.

"Mom! I did the whole thing. No script!" Arthur runs over to hug me. I smile at Leo over his head.

"That's awesome. You're totally ready."

Leo gets down from the couch and is all business. "Now the trick here is to stop practicing. You've got it and now you need to let it rest. Tonight you do whatever, eat your Tuesday food, do your homework." His eyes widen as he reaches for a bottle of wine. "I know. Tonight let's watch one of your mom's happy movies!"

Arthur rolls his eyes. "They're seriously dumb."

"I love them," offers Bernadette.

I appreciate the solidarity. "They are pretty dumb, but I love them too," I say. "Let's watch *Valentine Reunion*."

"Let me guess. High-powered female executive returns to her hometown and runs into her high school boyfriend."

"She's a professional pastry chef. But yes." We're all laughing, and Leo's handing me a glass of the most delicious wine ever.

＊　・　＊

LEO'S UP FOR the sunrise before I am. He's left a mug out for my coffee.

"Hey," he says.

"Thanks." I settle in next to him and take my mug. "So, this is your last Laurel Ridge sunrise."

"No. This is day six, which includes night six, which includes the sunrise tomorrow. What time's checkout?"

"We're pretty relaxed about that here." He looks at me with something that resembles gratitude, and I wonder if this time has done him any good.

"Are you glad you stayed? I mean, do you feel any better?"

"I feel pretty good. I was just thinking how much I miss being a part of a family. Like when I was growing up, we were this unit, and there was so much give-and-take. My brother, Luke, and I had to share food and space and attention. Now I barely see him, and my life's all about me. It's exhausting."

"Must be nice," I say out loud by mistake.

He gives me a nudge. "I know I sound like an asshole, but look at your life. You live for your kids, and they live for you. There's something almost sacred about what you have. In my life, I live for my career, and all the people around me are paid to live for my career. I swear last Thanksgiving I looked around my table and realized everyone there was on my payroll."

"Come on. You must have had some kind of normal relationship. Like with a woman who liked you and laughed at your lame jokes."

"Sure, tons. But the thing is they all liked me before they met me, like they fell in love with something they saw in *People* magazine. When my mom died, I thought: I just lost the last woman in the world who knew me. Of course, I don't bother getting to know them either."

"I met Ben so young that I never got to have that kind of quick meaningless relationship. Though I guess I had a long meaningless relationship instead." We both laugh at this, like Ben's an inside joke.

"This morning I woke up worried about Arthur. It was the strangest feeling to want something so much for someone else. You're really lucky."

I want to tell him he's welcome to stay, that maybe another week or two of this is just what he needs. But I know I'm on a slippery slope, because he's brought something with him, and he's going to take it when he leaves.

HE LEAVES ME alone all day, so that I have the tea house to myself from ten to two. My pencils are in position, and I haven't built a fire because it's warm outside. I listen to the birds through the open back windows. I sneak peeks through the front door to see if he's coming to see me.

I write garbage, more garbage-y than usual. Icky romantic scenes with long kisses and an otherwise sensible woman pouring her heart out. There's a marriage proposal at sunrise in the mountains, and well, I have officially lost my mind.

At one-thirty he's still not bothering me, so I decide to

take a nap. It's still my tea house, my daybed, so I figure I have the right to lie down. I don't dare get under his covers, that's way too personal, but I sink into his linen-covered pillow and smell his smell until I fall asleep.

There's a hand on my shoulder and a person sitting on the side of the bed. I've gone into one of those daytime stupors where you wake up and you don't know where you are. I blink at him. "Oh shit. Sorry. This is your bed. What time is it?"

"It's two-thirty. I came out to bring you some tea and you were passed out. I guess I was too late." He's really close to me. And I'm lying down. I don't know how I can sit up without getting even closer to him, so I just stay lying down.

"I was writing a lot of really terrible scenes. Bad writing wears me out." I'm still not entirely awake. "What have you been doing?"

"Pacing. Waiting for you to finish writing."

My stomach drops. "Oh?" is all I can muster.

"Yeah." He gets up and starts pacing the short length of the room. "I'm not sure about Arthur. I mean we were ready last night, but today, after a full day of school, he could have forgotten all of it. I mean, what if it's a disaster?"

Oh, sweet reality. Thank you. I sit up, scoot back, and comb my hair with my fingers. I am a person and a mother again. "Leo, he's ten. This is an elementary school play. Half the kids will throw up or start crying during the rehearsal. Arthur'll be fine."

"What time do we pick him up?"

"Oh my God. Okay." I stand up and take a deep breath.

"I'm really off my game. I'm in charge of the kids during rehearsal, like the ones waiting backstage." I check my phone. "I've got to go."

Leo follows me out. "I'm coming. You can't make me wait here."

"Fine. We'll leave in ten. I need to organize dinner."

"I'll do that. What do we eat on Wednesdays again?"

"Surprise me," I say.

I SWEAR WE are in slow motion walking past the pickup line into the front entrance of the school. I'd changed into a dress because I know for a fact it's three hundred degrees inside the auditorium on an April afternoon. "Legs!" Leo said as I came back down the stairs. On my advice, he changed from jeans into linen pants. Leo is absolutely focused, moving like we should have been there hours ago.

We pass through security ("he's my houseguest"), and we have to show our drivers' licenses. The security guard looks at Leo's and says, "For real?" Leo replies, "'Fraid so."

We meet Mrs. Sasaki in the auditorium. "Hi? I'm Nora Hamilton? Arthur's mom? We're here to watch the kids backstage?" I've met Mrs. Sasaki ten times and have never garnered much interest. Until now. Her eyes move from me to Leo and she actually smiles. "This is my friend Leo. We've been working together and he offered to help me with the kids, if that's okay?"

"Well, of course. Thank you! This is quite unexpected. Call me Brenda. We could use any help you can offer, Mr.

Vance. I heard you were in town. I daresay you know a little more about the theater than I do." Was she flirting with him? I look up at Leo to see how he's reacting, and he's smoldering. Smoldering poor Mrs. Sasaki. Poor Mrs. Sasaki who has to go home to poor Mr. Sasaki tonight. I swear Leo's going to ruin all of us for normal men.

As we make our way to the stage door, I say, "Stop it."

"What?"

"The smoldering."

He stops walking. "I don't smolder you."

I turn to face him, and I just ask it. "Why not?"

Leo holds my gaze. "I wish I knew."

Now, there's only so long you can stand that close to Leo Vance and look into his eyes without melting into molten lava, so I say, "Well, stop smoldering the other unsuspecting middle-aged ladies around here. Come on."

Bernadette meets us backstage to work as our assistant, but mainly to take a victory lap. No longer would anyone at Laurel Ridge Elementary question the fact that she is very good friends with The Leo Vance.

Arthur walks in, muttering lines to himself, and runs over to Leo. "What are you doing here?"

"Helping?" He shrugs. "You've got this, no worries. Just feel it, the whole thing. And eye contact."

We have the kids line up by scene according to the call list Mrs. Sasaki had given me. My job is pretty much to send the right group out on the stage and keep the rest of them quiet. The orphans are a little rowdy, showing off for the market girls, who are too preoccupied with Leo to notice.

The first time Arthur steps onstage, I lose Leo's help completely. He stands stage left, mouthing Arthur's lines and wringing his hands. Mrs. Sasaki stops Arthur to offer a suggestion; she'd like him to look out at the audience more while saying his lines.

"Okay." Arthur looks at Leo for confirmation.

"Don't you agree, Mr. Vance?"

"Well, I love the thought, Brenda. I do. And I really love it for his musical numbers. But in this scene, I think it's important that he connects with the orphans, that we can feel how he takes care of them. That's what'll grab the audience." Smolder.

He doesn't release her gaze until she finishes saying, "I see. I like that. What an absolutely helpful suggestion, Leo. Can I call you Leo?"

And, with that, Leo takes his place in the seat next to Mrs. Sasaki for the remainder of the rehearsal.

CHAPTER 8

T HERE'S A LARGE METAL BOX WAITING FOR US ON THE
porch, warming three brick oven pizzas from Mario's
in the city. On top is a bag with a huge chopped salad
and four cannoli. Apparently, Leo has taken care of dinner.

We plop down, exhausted, and tear into the pizza. Leo's
opened a bottle of pinot noir. Arthur and Bernadette are talking over each other. Who's any good, who can't dance. Who's
going to be thrown out of the production by Monday. Arthur
sits a little taller than usual, his quiet uncertainty morphing
into quiet confidence. It hasn't been the role in the play, I realize, it's been the attention and interest Leo's shown him. I
think Arthur feels supported.

Bernadette says the thing I cannot say. "So, tonight's your
last night?"

Leo looks at me, and I look at my wineglass. I don't know

what my face is doing but he doesn't need to see it. Arthur is silent.

"Well, this is awkward," he says. "I've been offered a job in town, co-director of *Oliver Twist*. I sort of promised Brenda I'd stay until opening night."

Bernadette squeals, and Arthur is still. "That's three weeks away," he says.

"It is." Leo fills both of our glasses.

"Well, that's nice of you," I start. "I mean, you want to do that? Of course, you can stay." I cannot be casual. I cannot find my normal voice.

"Thank you. Now, what's it time for? Homework?"

I PUTTER AROUND the kitchen, setting up the coffee maker for what will now not be Leo's last morning here. My relief is profound, but I'm clued in enough to know that it'll only be worse in three weeks when he leaves. And my kids, they adore him. I can't decide if it's healthy for my kids to know what it's like to have a man around who is interested in their lives, or if it's just going to make the pain they feel about Ben worse when Leo leaves. At least he's leaving us with something—a successful school-play memory. He's here for the play, and the duration of that play is finite. No one's going to be surprised when he goes.

I find Leo on the couch in the sunroom. He's opened a second bottle of wine and is looking out at the yard through open windows. "Join me?" he asks.

I grab another glass. Bernadette's art project is on the

armchair so I sit on the couch by his socked feet. "Thanks for letting me stay," he starts.

"Thanks for helping my kid."

He raises his glass in a toast, and I raise mine back and wait for him to speak. He puts it down. "I think toasting is really pretentious."

"Same."

"Do you think I should quit acting?"

I turn my whole body to him, pulling my legs onto the couch. "No. No one does. What are you talking about?"

"I don't know. I've made a lot of movies, and I'm only forty. I could have a whole second life, not being famous. Using the self-checkout gun."

"You're just burned out. You've made three movies in two years. This is a reset, and honestly, I'm really glad you're here. But you'll get excited about the next role, and you'll be back at it."

"I just sort of like doing this."

"You'd get sick of it."

"Are you?"

"Not at all."

He smiles. "Can I tell you a secret?"

I try to hide the excitement in my voice. "Sure."

"I've watched the Christmas movies on TRC. I love them."

"You do not." I try to contain the smile that is overtaking my face.

"I do. When I'm home for the holidays, my mom and I stay up late and watch two or three in a row. Or we did. She liked the young people falling in love; I like the overly wreathed houses and the moms cooking things. And everyone stressing about how the lights are hung." He takes a sip of his wine. "It's a guilty pleasure."

"What's your favorite?" *Pick one of mine! Pick one of mine!*

He considers this for longer than I think the question warrants. "The one where the reporter gets snowed in and stays to help the innkeeper plan the annual holiday festival. I liked the two of them; I felt like it made sense they'd be together."

"Becca and Daniel. Lake Placid. That's mine."

"See? You are romantic."

"Only on paper. And when the stakes are low."

CHAPTER 9

❧

B Y THE END OF FRIDAY AFTERNOON REHEARSALS, MRS.
Sasaki is pretty much just bringing Leo cups of water
and nodding at his ideas.

Weezie texts me as I am falling asleep: What's going on out
there? He says he's staying another three weeks???

I think it's restful for him here, I tell her.

Okay, then, I guess he's your problem. I'm going to "rest" in
his penthouse until I hear differently.

Good for you.

ON SATURDAY, LEO wants to come to Bernadette's soccer
game. He can't believe how many trees line the field and how
comfortable my stadium chairs are. He thinks Bernadette is

unusually aggressive for a girl her age and should have a private trainer before middle school. I roll my eyes a lot and try not to look at his feet. He's wearing flip-flops for the first time, I guess on account of the warmer weather. His feet are like his hands, strikingly beautiful but strong. I think of those feet walking up and down my stairs in the middle of the night. I try to never think about his hands.

My play-related problems are fixing themselves as Leo parades himself from the soccer field to the baseball field, shelling out hellos and smiles. We are twenty days from opening night and no one has volunteered to start working on sets or costumes. The backup plan was to have an old burlap curtain hanging on the stage and to have the children wear their dirtiest clothes, orphan style. Suddenly, everyone wants to be involved. In fact, they're swarming us.

Leo stands to his full height to meet Tanya Chung. He gazes deeply into her eyes until she agrees to have a full set of costumes by four P.M. a week from Wednesday, our first dress rehearsal. Evelyn Ness agrees to do all the sets, and I swear I saw her knees buckle a little.

"You'll never quit acting," I tell him.

"SO WHAT HAPPENS here on Saturday nights?" he asks us on the way home from Arthur's extra-innings disastrous Little League game.

"I have a sleepover at Sasha's," says Bernadette.

"I have a birthday party," says Arthur.

"Oh, looks like we're out of luck. Can I take you out to dinner?"

Giggles from the back seat and now I might be blushing. I crack the window. "Sure."

"Someplace decent?"

"We have a bistro in town that's very good. Don't be a snob."

Leo rolls his eyes in the rearview mirror to more giggles.

I THINK I'M wearing too much makeup, but I have no one to ask. I'm not comfortable with black stuff on my eyes, and I feel mildly like an assault victim. But it seems rude not to make a little effort on a Saturday night, so I pick my navy blue silk dress, the one with no sleeves in case I sweat.

My hair is right today, thank God for small favors. "You're a grown-up person," I tell my reflection. "Don't act like a teenager."

"Damn," he says as I walk into the kitchen. He's in a crisp white shirt and a navy blazer. He's shaved and smiling, and well, he looks like a movie star.

"Too much?" I really just need someone to be honest with me.

"Just right."

As expected, we walk into the restaurant and everyone takes a collective gasp. People who know me even in passing give enthusiastic waves. People who know me well plot their frequent trips to the bathroom so they can stop and say hi.

The hostess takes us to a table in the back corner, facing out into the restaurant. Leo puts his hand on her forearm and she almost faints. "I don't want to be a pain, but would it be possible to seat us at that table over there?" He motions to a table nestled in front of a banquette.

After one glass of wine, I forget that my entire community is staring at us. We're laughing about how he charmed those poor women into working on the play. We talk about the kids, like they're a shared interest of ours. He wants to know about my brief career in publishing, and his responses make me realize I learned more than I thought.

"Do you date?" he wants to know.

"No."

"Never?"

"Never."

"Why not?"

"These are some pretty rural suburbs. Singles don't exactly congregate here. Plus, I get up early, as you know."

"Are you ever lonely?"

"Not as lonely as I was when I was married to Ben."

When our desserts come, he wants to play his new favorite game, Romance Movie. "Okay, here's one. Male talk-show host from Akron, Ohio."

I stab a bite of chocolate cake as I think. "He goes out to the country to interview a reclusive movie star and falls for her caregiver, who probably dreams of opening a cupcake shop."

"They all do."

"An inordinate number of bakers in these movies," I agree. "And no one's overweight."

"Community activity at the end?"

"Hmm." I take a bite and think it over. "Oh. He's going to MC the auction for the county fair."

"Where she'll be selling cupcakes."

"Naturally."

"And he has to leave before the event, breaks her heart but then comes back and there's a big kiss," he says.

"The kiss is never really that big, actually."

He's finished his wine, so I pour him half of mine. "So that's it?" he asks.

"Well, there's small stuff. If either of them has parents, they're always exceptionally loving and self-sufficient. No one's parents are a pain." I take another bite of cake. "And the woman usually has a quirk that would be annoying to most men, but that this particular guy finds irresistible."

"Seriously?"

"It's part of the fantasy. Like the woman who's really uptight and makes tons of lists appeals to the musician who needs to get his act together."

"This is diabolical. What about the lunatic woman who schedules her life to run like a Swiss watch?"

"Well," I say, draining my glass and placing my napkin on the table, "she gets a lot of shit done. But, in my experience, it's not exactly the kind of thing a man finds irresistible."

"I do," he says. "We should go home."

THE HOUSE IS dark when we get back and neither of us switches on a light. We're just standing there in the dark kitchen, and he takes a step toward me. "Do we need to pick up Arthur?"

Arthur? I wonder. Oh right. "Kate's giving him a ride home."

"Okay," he says. He's close enough that if he took half a step forward he could kiss me. I wonder again if my imagination has gone rogue, if maybe it's time to lay off the romance genre. And the wine.

"My salmon was perfectly cooked," I say literally out of nowhere, mainly because I need to break eye contact. I sidestep so we're no longer facing each other. "I mean sometimes it's too rare, and they say pink in the middle, but it's practically still breathing. Not that fish breathe." I laugh a little at my truly unfunny comment, but now I can breathe. I turn to the counter and start straightening an already straight stack of papers in the dark. "Want to get that light?" I say.

"No," he says and steps right behind me.

"Oh," I say, turning around.

He moves a loose tendril of hair from my eyes and rests his hand on the side of my neck. I can't remember his having touched me before, and from the tingly heat spreading through my body, I think I would have remembered. I cannot look him in the eye, but I can feel him studying me in the dark. He leans in, and his face is so close that our noses brush against each other. His breath is on my lips. The space between us is electric with want, mostly mine probably, and I'm afraid to meet his eyes because he'll see all that want, laid bare. For some reason I want to stay in this moment, ride this

NORA GOES OFF SCRIPT

line, so I can both know and not know what's about to happen. It will be the Schrödinger's cat of kisses.

He whispers my name and moments pass. I finally raise my eyes to his, and Leo kisses me. First a small, testing kiss and then an endless kiss that dissolves me. He is kissing me with such urgency that I want to believe he's been imagining this as often as I have. There is nothing in the world more natural or inevitable than his hands on my hips, my hands in his hair. I don't know where I am when headlights are pulling into my driveway. A car door opens and closes, and Leo mutters, "Arthur."

Leo hits the light as Arthur's coming through the front door. We're both a little breathless, so I say, "Hey, honey, perfect timing, we just came up from the garage." Even though my car's parked out front. "How was it?"

"Good. We watched a movie and played Nerf wars in the woods behind their house." He gets himself a glass of water, and we watch, maybe not wanting to look at each other. "Well, good night," he says and gives us each a hug.

"Good night, sweetie. I'll be right up to tuck you in." I say this because it's what I say. Every single night. There is no part of me that wants to leave this kitchen.

When we can hear the water running upstairs, Leo takes my hand and entwines our fingers. "Well," he says.

"Yeah." I can't stop looking at our hands together. His hand right there, all mixed up with mine.

"I guess I'll turn in too?" he says.

"Okay."

"Okay," he says and he kisses me again, just the tiniest tease of a kiss. "I'll see you for sunrise," he says and walks out the back door, across the lawn to the tea house.

I BARELY SLEEP, of course. I text Penny: I hope I'm not waking you, but if I am can you still text me back? He kissed me.

I text the same thing to Kate. I get no response. My heart is racing, and I need to talk myself down. Fact: I will probably never recover from that kiss. Fact: This is a man who dates starlets. Fact: I am a regular woman who's nursed two babies. Oh, dear God. Maybe he was drunk. He didn't seem drunk. Maybe he's acting. He seemed sincere. Maybe he's just acting sincere. For what? To steal a few kisses from a lonely suburban mom? He's really been playing the long con if that was his angle. He could kiss anyone he wanted. *Maybe he really likes me,* I think in my tiniest thinking voice.

When the light starts to fill my room, I open my eyes and remember. I jump out of bed and analyze my pajama situation. White flannel with little yellow stars. I swap out my pajama top for a T-shirt and throw a light blue sweater over it. My neck looks weird so I add a scarf. When I see the whole look together, I realize that I've done it again. I look like my giveaway pile threw up on me. I change back into straight pajamas.

I enter the kitchen and see the coffee's already been brewed. He's left a mug out for me. I pour my coffee and make my way out.

"You're late," he says. I sit, and he covers me with his

blanket. I look for signs that something's changed, that this is a more intimate gesture. But it's the same way he's shared his blanket since the first day, a thousand years ago, back when my nightgown was see-through. I am oddly aware of my lips on my coffee mug. They feel like ordinary lips, but they're not because they were kissed by Leo Vance last night. I don't want to look at him, because I know I'll be staring at his lips.

We watch the sky as the leaves are backlit by the sun. The show's almost over, and I need to hear him say something, anything that will indicate that this actually happened and that he plans to kiss me again.

"What's the schedule today?" he asks. Ah, romance. The mention of "the schedule" feels like a blow, like maybe I thought he was going to suggest eloping to Cap d'Antibes. *What's the schedule today?* It takes me a beat to remember that it's Sunday, and I shake my head clear.

Deep breath. "It's Sunday," I say to buy time. "Bernadette has a soccer game at one, and it's an hour away in Yardsmouth. Arthur has another birthday party, a noon movie."

"Is Yardsmouth any good?" Ugh. He's clearly grasping at any possible topic that doesn't relate to that kiss. Girls U9 soccer will certainly do the trick.

"They're terrible. It won't be much of a game."

"Interesting," he says.

I'm a little vulnerable. I've opened myself up to the possibility that this kiss was a real thing, the beginning of a thing. And here he is staring straight ahead, talking about the household calendar. Soon he'll be asking about how the Crockpot works and if you should wash dark clothes in hot water.

"Not really," I say. I pull my legs up into my chest. I ache, and I'm a little mad. You can't just go around kissing lonely women for no reason. It's irresponsible and borderline cruel. It's like giving a dog a steak one day and then switching back to kibble the next. You don't know what you don't know, and that kiss wasn't something I needed to know about.

"Is there any way to get Bernadette a ride to Yardsmouth?"

"Why?" I'm still not looking at him.

"Because if we did, we could be alone here from eleven-thirty to two." He's looking at me now.

I flush, like actually flush. "Oh," I say.

"Can we?"

"I'll call Jenna," I say. I still haven't looked at him, but he reaches for my hand under the blanket. Like that's the most normal thing in the world.

CHAPTER 10

I'M CAREFUL NOT TO MAKE EYE CONTACT WITH LEO THROUGH-out breakfast. I can feel him watching me, but I can't risk my kids seeing whatever lustful madness might cross my face if we lock eyes. I make an overly complicated breakfast of from-scratch waffles and sausage. I go for a slightly longer than usual run and find that I have burned off zero percent of my nervous energy. I shower and dress and head back down-stairs. I've caught Arthur's attention.

"Do you have something today?"

I stop on the stairs. I look at him and then, finally, at Leo. "Why?"

"That dress. Do you have a party?"

I look down at my yellow sundress, and I don't really have an explanation. My regular T-shirt and jeans uniform didn't seem good enough today. Maybe on some unconscious level I think jeans are hard to get off and leave seam lines on your skin? I silently curse myself for showing my hand.

"Oh, I'm a little behind on laundry. Why don't you grab Howie's gift and I'll drop you at the movie theater."

"Mom. It's only ten-thirty."

"Right." Leo's at the kitchen counter pretending to read something on his phone, but I catch him stifling a laugh.

AFTER JENNA'S COME for Bernadette and we hear her car pull onto the main road, Leo crosses the kitchen and takes me into his arms. With my body on high alert, I realize that I am badly in need of this hug. The strength of his arms around me and the reassuring smell of him is starting to calm me down.

"So where are we right now?" he says into my hair.

"I'm terrified," I admit.

"Me too. Can I take you out to the tea house?"

It feels like the right idea, to get away from the smell of waffles and stacks of dishes into a space where we can think more clearly. "Sure," I say, and he takes my hand as we walk barefoot outside.

When we're inside, he shuts the door. I'm not sure where to be so I sit down on his unmade bed. Leo doesn't join me.

"Want me to make a fire?"

"It's pretty warm in here."

"Right." He straightens the chair at the table. He folds a sweater that had been hanging on the back. It feels like he's stalling. I scoot back on the bed and curse the dress choice again. I want to bring my knees to my chest in a protective posture so that I can feel safe while I discern what's happening here. Out of propriety, I can only sit crisscross-applesauce, which leaves me feeling childish and exposed.

"Can I come sit with you?" he asks.

"Of course." He walks the two steps to the bed and sits down carefully, like the placement of his body might accidentally detonate a bomb.

I need to touch him and I am starting to worry this might be my last chance. I take his hand in mine and I run my fingers over his palm. I'll do this forever to avoid hearing him say this was a mistake.

I say, "I know why I'm terrified. What are you so nervous about? Don't you do this all the time?" I'm trying to lighten things up, like we're just Nora and Leo shooting the breeze, but it falls flat.

"You're a real person."

"Because I drive a Subaru?" I'm not sure when I developed this knack for bringing up the world's least sexy things at the worst possible times.

"Because I know you. I don't have a lot of experience with that."

"Well, I don't have a lot of experience at all," I say.

"We don't have to do this." He says this, but now his hand is on the inside of my crossed ankle. He's studying the line he's drawing up the length of my calf. The feel of his fingers barely touching my skin as they reach the back of my knee makes me catch my breath.

"I think we do," I say, almost in a whisper because I don't trust my voice. He looks up and kisses me deeply, gripping his hands behind my head, as if I'm a flight risk. As if. I am so dizzy with this kiss that I don't know when my arms wrap around his neck and my legs find their way around his back. The dress, as it turns out, was a good decision. We are in a frenzy of clothing removal, and when there is nothing between us, everything but my heart rate slows down. He kisses me slowly, and as he starts to make love to me, I know for sure that Leo hasn't been acting. In his rawest state, with his guard completely down, he is the same person who's been sitting on my porch—attentive, listening, staying for the whole story. For the first time in my life, I have left my busy, busy mind and now exist only in the smell of Leo's neck. The sound of Leo whispering my name. The slick of his skin now damp with sweat. The feeling of my body opening up to something so powerful I don't know how I'll return from it.

The daybed's too small for us to lie side by side afterward, so I turn my back to Leo to gather my thoughts. *Where are my thoughts?* Leo turns and wraps his arms around me, kisses the back of my neck. I'm feeling a little embarrassed. I have never in my life been this exposed.

"I've been thinking about that for a long time," he says.

"You only met me two weeks ago."

Leo laughs and kisses my shoulder. "You really aren't very romantic, are you?"

"I might be an overthinker."

"I'll fix you," he says, and I turn around to face him. He's joking, but I love the idea of being on the other side of the fixing equation. I love the idea that he thinks I'm worth the trouble. I love that buried deep in that sentence is a hint of the future tense.

MY KIDS KNOW something's up, but mercifully they don't know what. They're at an age where their first suspicion wouldn't be sex, but they're also at an age where they are exquisitely tuned in to subtle changes in their mother. I feel them watching me, and I don't know if it's the lightness in my body or the smile on my face while I wash potatoes. I know I'm glowing, and there's nothing I can do to hide that or make it stop.

While everything's changed, in that first week my routine isn't so different. Sunrise, breakfast, kids to school, run, shower, tea house from ten to two. Except instead of writing, I lie in bed with a movie star. There's a lot of sex, like a ridiculous amount of sex. In my previous life, I would have considered half this amount of sex to be a complete nightmare, but now a day spent in bed feels like a day well spent. It's possible that I didn't really understand what sex was before Leo.

I used to think about the plumber a lot when I had sex with Ben. Not because I was in any way attracted to the plumber, but more because I'd wonder if I'd called to have him check the seal on the outdoor water spigot. If I hadn't, the pipes might freeze and burst, and that would be really pricey. A fix like that would bite into my already tight Christmas budget. And I really needed to convince Arthur that he doesn't need a drum set. Forget the noise, but just the amount of space it would take up and how much it would irritate me to vacuum around it when he was sick of it by New Year's. On New Year's Day, I like making a curried chicken salad, but Arthur's doctor has repeatedly told us that he might want to cut back on dairy. I'd have to break that tradition because of the mayonnaise. But, wait. Mayonnaise is just oil and eggs. There's no dairy in mayonnaise! Arthur can have all he wants! I could even make macaroni salad and that vegetable dip he likes. *Mayonnaise isn't dairy,* I'd smile to myself as Ben rolled off of me. Of course, Ben thought that smile, like everything else, was about him.

I guess the problem with Ben in bed was the same as the problem with Ben out of bed: Ben's all about Ben. Ben is focused exclusively on what's going to make Ben happy, what's going to make Ben feel good, and what's going to reflect well on Ben to the outside world. With Leo, it's not about either of us. It's like there's this third thing we've created. We step into that space and the rest of the world is gone. There is no time, no news, no world outside that daybed until three o'clock.

Leo likes to run his finger from the bottom of my ear, down my neck, and along my collarbone, and sometimes the rhythm of it puts me to sleep. We get up for food deliveries. Sometimes we run errands. We are at once energized and lazy, supercharged and sleepy. I wonder if other people can feel that we are operating on a different energetic wave, like we hear a separate soundtrack and feel the air on our skin in a more exquisite way. Deep down, I'm fully aware that this is not a sustainable reality, but I cling to it like you do with a really good dream when you're sure you could never replicate the feeling in real life.

Leo has never set foot in my bedroom. He doesn't so much

as brush his hand against mine when my kids are home. We don't discuss this, but he seems to understand my instinct to protect them. In the darkest corner of my being, where a tiny piece of me still recognizes reality, I know Leo is temporary. I'm in for a horrible fall, but as long as I can keep that as my problem, not theirs, this is worth it.

He starts coming on my runs, which he says are boring. I like a loop because it forces me to finish. And, frankly, my whole life is a loop; every day I end up right where I began. He likes variety, so we start exploring the back country roads that wind around Laurel Ridge. Some stretches are paved and some are dirt, changing up that sound our feet make as we run. We pass an occasional house with a split-rail fence, but mostly the roads have meadows on both sides, lined with the last of the daffodils. Old cherry trees and dogwoods offer sporadic shade, and if the wind blows at just the right time, we run through a shower of white blossoms that feel like confetti.

Sometimes we run so far out that we walk back, and sometimes he holds my hand. We are in the middle of a days-long conversation that winds around the most inconsequential and most monumental details of our lives.

"So, my mom had lung cancer," he tells me on a walk. "But they didn't tell me until the very end. They didn't want to interrupt my filming, like that matters." He's quiet for a while. "I finally saw her the day before she died. Luke had been there for two weeks, which really pissed me off. The last thing she ever said to me was 'movie stars don't do hospice.'"

"What does Luke do?" I ask.

"Luke's a lawyer. I guess lawyers do hospice. Anyway, in

ANNABEL MONAGHAN

three days I found out she was sick, said good-bye, and she died."

"So that's why you're here?" I hate the neediness in my voice the second I say it.

"You're why I'm here," he says. "But before you, this, it felt good to connect to real life—the forest, the sunrise, the schedule. Like a person who knows about that stuff can totally handle hospice."

Later, in the tea house, he wants to know more about Ben. "There must be something very, very wrong with him," he says and kisses me so softly that I might start to cry.

He knows most of the story, because he played him in the movie. How we met in college and moved to the city. How I got a job in publishing and he was going to start a tech company. How a year into his start-up, a bigger company launched the same project. How the same thing happened with his next idea, and the next. The movie doesn't cover the real money stuff—how Ben blew through any money I made almost aggressively. Like he shopped out of anger.

"I guess because he was raised rich, he never expected anything to be hard. He literally couldn't handle it if things didn't go his way. Like he was owed."

"What happened to the grandfather's money?"

"It was all mismanaged over the years; Ben's dad didn't really focus on the business when it was his turn to run it. So what's left is a bunch of angry, entitled people with no money who don't know how to take care of themselves."

"You should have put that in the movie. I would have

liked that for his character, like it was hard for me to understand why Trevor was such a tool."

I move Leo's hair out of his eyes. "It was my fault too. I
let him pretend he was about to hit it big. I covered for him
for years because I didn't want to be wrong about my marriage, my life."

"You're a chump," he kids. "I should tell you, I'm not
good with money either. I don't know anything about it."

"Except that you can afford a lot of bananas."

Leo laughs. "So many bananas."

"Well, I'm rich now, so it's all good," I say.

"You are? All my dreams have come true." He pulls me in
tight. "What a catch."

"I'm serious. *The Tea House* got me out of debt. When
you've been in a lot of debt, having no debt feels pretty rich.
This isn't going to be the movie where the heroine has to sell
the farm."

"Thank God. I like the farm."

"One day, Ben found me in here sorting through a stack of
bills, trying to figure out which ones we needed to pay and
which ones we could lag on. I said something about how we'd
be better off if we both had jobs. And I think that was the
end. On that day, I think he added me to the list of people
who were getting in the way of his big dreams."

"That was actually in the movie."

I laugh, because it all is a blur. Real life made into a movie
that turns into a wild affair with the man who pretended to be
my husband on-screen. For a person whose life is pretty

straightforward, I never thought all my story lines would loop back in on one another.

"Did you love him?"

"Maybe early on. But there are parts of people you can't unsee after years of living with them. Well, his disinterest in the kids, for one. But also his total self-obsession, his inability to appreciate beauty. Lots of things."

"I appreciate beauty," he says. And he smiles a smile I don't know from the movies. It's the same one he had when Arthur made it all the way through his script without looking.

"What's this smile?" I ask, tracing his lips.

"I'm happy. I'm so happy he left you."

PENNY TEXTS ME ten times a day: What's happening now? How long is he staying? Why aren't you texting me back????? I reply: I am dangerously happy and generally too naked to text you back.

For two hours every afternoon, we are apart and it's excruciating. He's in the auditorium playing director, and I'm backstage babysitting. It's odd to see all the normal people treating me like a normal person. I am not a normal person. I'm Leo Vance's girlfriend.

"Mrs. Hamilton," Savanah asks, "are we practicing the market scene today?" *I don't know,* I think. *I don't even know what day it is.* It hasn't even been a week since Leo became my lover, and I'm in a fog that I don't want lifted.

Kate is helping me corral the kids and calls them out in groups to get outfitted for costumes. I let her take over. "I have never seen you like this," she says.

"Like what?" As if I don't know.

"Giddy. Loose. Spacey."

"I am all of those things."

"So like, what's the plan? He's staying a couple of weeks and then leaving after the first performance?"

"Well, that's what he said before, but now I don't know. We don't talk about it, but he kind of talks like he's staying. Like there's more than this." Her look of concern is hard to ignore. "I'm totally delusional, aren't I?"

"No, my friend, you are in love. We just don't see what the happy ending looks like yet." She puts her arm around me and gives me a squeeze.

SOMETIMES I LEAVE the kids with Kate so that I can stand at stage left and watch Leo direct. First of all, I just like looking at him. And if I'm lucky I'll catch his eye and he'll shoot me a look that makes me shiver. I also like to see Leo doing what he does, trying to teach the kids about acting. He takes the whole thing so seriously.

Leo seems to think that Oliver is phoning it in. He's squatting down in front of Ty Jackson's unusually small frame and looking him right in the eye. "I need you to get into Oliver's head."

Ty just stares at him. "His head?"

"I need you to imagine his circumstances. You have no parents, no home."

"I have a swimming pool," Ty tells him.

"You do. But Oliver doesn't. I need you to imagine your

parents are gone and you have nothing but the clothes you are wearing right now. You don't have a blanket to keep you warm. Not one single friend." Twelve other cast members look on as Ty closes his eyes and tries to imagine. Twelve other cast members are horrified when Ty bursts into tears.

Leo puts his arms around Ty. "That's it. Use that in this next scene."

I rush out and say, "Let's take a little break." *Too far,* I mouth to Leo.

When the kids are getting picked up from rehearsal, Leo walks Ty out to find his mother. The kids and I stay a few feet behind, as if this is either highly personal or highly professional and we shouldn't be seeing.

"Hey, I'm Leo," he says, sticking his hand out to Ty's mom, who seems to be unable to control her smile. "I think I owe Ty here an apology, and I wanted you to know."

"What? Oh, I'm sure he's fine. We just can't get over the fact that you're directing this play. Never in a million years." Ty has both of his arms around his mom's waist.

"I made him cry. And I'm really sorry." To Ty, "You're such a good actor, I forgot you're ten. Forget all that stuff I said, okay? You were doing it perfect before."

Ty lets go of his mom and hugs Leo. "Okay," he says.

"YOU'VE JUST GOT to own up," Leo says at dinner, gnawing on a chicken bone. "If you do it enough, it's not even that hard. 'I blew it, I'm sorry.' It's not such a big deal."

"I really thought Ty was going to lose it," says Arthur.

NORA GOES OFF SCRIPT

"It's the only way. When you screw up, you've got to make it right," says Leo. "This is my dad's favorite thing to talk about—personal responsibility. If you own up to not being perfect, life gets easier. And let's face it, I was totally off base. I don't know anything about kids. You guys are the only kids I know."

I wonder if my kids are thinking about Ben. I wonder if they ever noticed how he'd double down on every misstep just to avoid admitting he was wrong. I hope they can't see on my face how absolutely in love with Leo I am in this moment. I hope that, while I can no longer be saved from myself, they are taking this at face value: We have a nice houseguest who's helping with the play and sharing his worldview. But I have to admit that the four of us around the kitchen table feels like something much more than that.

"I'm embarrassed when I have to say sorry. Like I feel all hot inside," says Bernadette.

"Then you should keep doing it until it's easy," says Leo. "But only when you're actually wrong."

"I don't think Ty's going to be a very good Oliver," says Arthur.

"Me neither," says Leo. "But we gotta let that go and just do the best we can."

Arthur nods at Leo, like with a profound understanding. Something is happening over chicken and rice and green beans. Wisdom is being exchanged. Some might call it parenting. I marvel at the fact that this moment was created by someone besides me. Even when Ben was here, I used to wake up in the middle of the night worrying that every life lesson my kids would ever get would come from me. Do they know how to cross the street? Do they know to run in a zigzag if they're being chased by a bear? The lessons they'd learn from Ben would be more like cautionary tales: Don't be an entrepreneur if you don't want to work at it. Don't belittle your kids if you want them to love you.

Leo smiles at me over his wineglass. We clean up; we watch *Wheel of Fortune*. He insists that I go up and read to them and tuck them in. He goes out to the tea house and we text until we both fall asleep. This routine is preposterous really. I barely sleep, and I haven't written a word since that first kiss. But I don't want a single thing to change.

CHAPTER II

MOST MORNINGS, WE SNUGGLE OUR WAY THROUGH the sunrise and listen for the creak of the screen door. It's a Saturday, but Bernadette is not a late sleeper. "Move over," she commands before she's all the way outside. She sits next to Leo, and he puts his arm around her. She leans into his chest. I haven't noticed this before and wonder if it's the first time. I can't make my mind compute how long Leo's been here, but suddenly it feels like he always has been.

"What's on for today?" he asks her.

"I have soccer; Arthur has a baseball game. But there's a food truck festival at Craft Park. We should go."

"I'm there," says Leo.

"You will be swarmed," I tell him.

"I've been swarmed before," he says. "You guys can protect me."

We get through soccer (a success) and baseball (less so) and head straight to the festival. It's packed. There are ten food trucks and at least twenty people in each line. There's a band playing country songs and a station with kegs. Besides the fact that I am getting out of a crappy station wagon with my two kids, I feel young and light.

"Want a beer?" my boyfriend asks.

"Sure," I say. My kids run off and I stand there watching him. He gets in the back of the beer line, hands in his jeans pockets, until one and then two and then ten people notice him and turn around. Based on his body language, he seems perfectly fine with it. Soon the whole line is in conversation with him, laughing in turns. A little girl hands him a pen and a paper bag, and he signs it. As the line moves, he almost seems like he's keeping the conversation going, asking questions, nodding. The lady from the too-fancy-housewares shop joins the group, and they exchange a few words.

I imagine him coming to this thing year after year, remembering names and key facts about everybody, watching the kids grow up. He'd cry at Mr. Mapleton's funeral and remember how he'd just met him after he got the new hip. "She's stoned," someone is saying, and I snap out of it to see Kate and Mickey standing next to me.

"I am not," I say. "Just lost in a daydream of sorts."

"And here he comes," says Mickey, nodding at Leo making his way back to us with two plastic cups of beer. "How am I ever going to compete with this?" Mickey's a firefighter in town and maybe the best guy I've ever met. Neither Kate nor I feel the need to reassure him.

"Hey, Kate." Leo hands me my beer and shakes Mickey's hand. "I'm Leo."

"Well, you seem to handle a crowd pretty well," says Mickey. "If I were you, I might have just stayed in the car."

"Oh, it was fine. I knew half of them from my shopping spree in town. Nora makes me buy her a lot of stuff."

I give him a shove and he puts his arm around me. I hear Mickey say to Kate, "Wow. You weren't kidding."

"Are you guys free tonight?" Leo asks. "We were going to barbecue and I'm sure we have a lot? Or I could go to the market?" He is asking me for guidance here, and I am slightly stunned to see him acting like we're a couple and we share a barbecue.

"That's a great idea," I say. "Bring the kids. Come at five?"

LEO IS DISAPPOINTED that I have enough food and he doesn't get to go to the market. Bernadette thinks we should eat out on the lawn in front of the tea house. I try not to watch as she and Leo remove the legs from my kitchen table to move it outside.

When I get back from taking Arthur to town to get grip tape for his bat, Leo and Bernadette are waiting for me on the front porch. "We need your car," Bernie says. In an hour they are back with a yellow-and-white-striped tablecloth, matching napkins, and six strands of white lights. I can barely see Bernadette behind the enormous bouquet of sunflowers she's carrying.

"I'm on-set design," she tells me.

"Have you guys lost your minds?" I ask as they get to work.

"A little." Leo shoots me a smile.

There's no way Arthur and I spent as much time preparing the food as they spend setting the scene. Leo's found a ladder and some twine. They hang the lights between the trees on either side of the lawn, making a long sparkling ceiling over the table. Even before the sun goes down, it is breathtaking.

When dinner's over, and the kids are playing Wiffle ball in the front yard, Kate and I are aggressively filling Mickey's wineglass. We are not discussing this, but we both want him to feel comfortable and maybe get past the fact that he doesn't think Leo really works for a living.

Kate's telling stories about her work. She runs a nonprofit parenting program for people living in underserved communities. The program runs on almost no budget and the sheer force of her will, and the stunts she pulls to make ends meet are heroic. Leo is asking all the right questions that indicate that he is listening to every word she says, making Kate more animated and forthcoming than I've ever seen her. This is Leo's superpower, and it's possible that it's getting on Mickey's nerves.

Leo and I sit facing the tea house and the forest behind it, and he says to no one, "It's so beautiful here. It's like every day something new has bloomed."

"Wait till July when the hydrangea come in," Kate says. "They'll blow your mind." The word "July" hangs in the air.

Kate and I lock eyes and I look away. Mickey is leaning back in his chair watching Leo.

Leo doesn't miss a beat. "Can't wait," he says. He squeezes my hand, and I know in that moment that I want Leo and those hydrangea blooms to be in the same place at the same time more than anything else. It scares me how much I want him to stay.

"So where are you from?" Mickey starts his interrogation.

"New Jersey," Leo says. "Exit Eighty-two."

Mickey laughs, and I'm not sure if that's nice. "And now you live in Los Angeles?"

"And New York," he says.

"And Cap d'Antibes," I say and roll my eyes.

"Yeah, I can see why you spend so much time in Laurel Ridge, must be a nice break," Mickey says.

"It's pretty good," Leo says and puts his arm around the back of my chair.

Kate smiles at us, and everyone's quiet for a second until Mickey says, "I just don't know what the hell is going on here. Like, are you staying? You're just going to live here? How do you know you won't get sick of this?"

"Mickey." Kate swats him with her napkin. "Get it together. It's none of our business."

"Nora's none of our business?" I see now that he's been overserved. "I fucking hated Ben," he says to Leo. "He was arrogant and lazy."

"Sounds like he was a crappy dad too," Leo says.

"How much money did you make last year?" Mickey asks,

ANNABEL MONAGHAN

like it's nothing. Kate swats him again, and I shake my head at Leo, who doesn't flinch.

"I have no idea, but you could probably google it."

Mickey laughs and holds up his beer to Leo. "Must be nice."

"It is. You get used to not thinking about money pretty quick. But, like they say, it won't make you happy."

"It'd make me happy," says Mickey.

"That's because you're already happy."

122

CHAPTER 12

O N MONDAY MY PHONE RINGS AT ABOUT NOON.
We're in the tea house, and it's Ben. Leo and I stare
at it for a few seconds. "Do you want to get it?" he
asks.

"Do you?" I put the phone down and turn over. There's
no way I want to let Ben into this cocoon.

"I mean, could it be important? He doesn't usually call,
does he?"

I turn back to Leo, and the phone has mercifully stopped
ringing. "He calls every few months. He says he wants to see
the kids. I say 'great!' Then he says he'll call back later in the
week when he's 'nailed down a few deets.' And then he never
calls."

"Never?"

"Never. The first time, I told the kids that he was coming,
and they were all excited. But of course he didn't come, so

now I don't tell them. On the off chance he ever knocks on the door, it'll just be a surprise."

The phone's ringing again. Leo says, "He's calling back? Seriously, you should pick up."

"He just doesn't like being ignored," I say, and I answer the call on speakerphone.

"Hi, Ben."

"Hey there. How's it going?"

"Great." I smile at Leo, because it is going great, so great, beyond great in my wildest fantasies, if I'd ever taken the time to have any.

"Great. And how are the kids?"

"They're good. I mean, their dad left and he never sees them. But otherwise they're good."

"Do you realize you say that every single time we talk?"

"I do."

He lets out an exasperated breath. "So, I was thinking I'd come in two weeks. I just have to nail down a few deets, but is it okay if I come and take them for a weekend?"

"Sure." Leo rolls his eyes, and I nod.

"Okay, thanks. So you're good? You sound a little distracted. Working on another one of your corny romances?"

I smile at Leo. "I am. And this is the best, corniest one yet."

"Ha. Ever finish the one you were writing about me?"

"I did." Leo's making big eyes at me.

"Hilarious," Ben says, because he really has no idea what a jerk he is.

When I hang up, Leo pulls me in tight. "So there's no chance he's going to follow through and show up?"

"I would drop dead of shock if he knocked on the door. Let me put it this way: Ben always does what he wants to do. If he wants something, he buys it. If he wants to leave, he goes. If he wanted to see the kids, he would have been here months ago."

"Just do me a favor. Let me answer the door if he ever knocks," Leo says.

THE WEEK ROLLS by in a familiar rhythm. Wake, sunrise, kids, run, tea house, play rehearsal, dinner. Some days we act like a normal couple. We go to the supermarket and the little grocery in town. He wants to go to Costco, but I tell him he can't handle it. We go to lunch at the bistro and sit at the same table as our first date. I am so comfortable with Leo that I sometimes think I've lost the ability to pause between thinking something and saying something.

The waiter brings my bouillabaisse, and I say, "Are you really going to leave after opening night?" I can't believe I've said it once it's out. I look at my clams and try to regain my cool. "I mean, I know that's the plan, but is it still the plan?"

Leo says, "I don't have any place I need to be."

Relief. "Okay. Well, good. I mean I didn't know if I should be counting down or . . . oh, for chrissake." Vicky freakin' Miller walks into the restaurant.

"What?"

"It's Vicky Miller. She had an affair with Ben and thinks I don't know. Which is ridiculous because everyone in town knows."

"That bastard," he says. "What the hell."

"Deep down, Ben felt really, really bad about himself."

"You're still covering for him."

And in an instant, there's Vicky standing at the side of our table, big smile. "Nora! I can't believe it. I never see you out!" Nice.

"It must be Groundhog Day," I say, making like I'm peering out of my hole.

"I'm Leo," says Leo, with more reserve than I'm used to.

"Yes. I'm Vicky," she says, like that's exciting news. "I heard you were making a movie in town."

"I was. But now I'm just staying with Nora." He reaches across the table and takes my hand, waiting for her to speak.

"Well, that's nice," says Vicky, who left her underwear in my husband's Audi.

When we've left the restaurant, Leo has a thousand questions. "So you never confronted him about it? You never confronted her?"

"I'm not a big confronter. I mean, it was clear he didn't love me anymore, and it's not like you can talk someone into loving you again."

"Did you want him to love you again?"

I have to consider this for a second. "I guess. If he loved me it would have meant I was a good wife, that I'd been adequate at keeping our world spinning. I liked the idea of that.

NORA GOES OFF SCRIPT

But I didn't really care too much about the affair. A year later, he was gone anyway, so no harm, no foul."

Leo stops me on the sidewalk. "That's just cold. It didn't hurt a little?"

"Well, a little. But what was I supposed to do? I kind of had a lot on my plate."

"Tell me this. If I went and had sex with stupid Vicky whoever, would you care?" A woman wheels a stroller around us, but Leo's not budging. "Just tell me. I know how to make a scene."

"Why are you asking?"

"I'm just gathering information." Leo is vulnerable in this moment. His face is expectant and his shoulders are braced as if he's expecting a blow.

"I'd care a lot," I say. And he kisses me, right there on the sidewalk at two o'clock in the middle of town.

As we walk to the car, he's laughing. "I knew it. You're so into me."

MICKEY HAS TAKEN to stopping by on his way home from work to have a beer with Leo. Apparently, Leo won him over at the barbecue. There's something about the way Leo is so comfortable with his success that makes it easy for you to forget about it. By the time Mickey and Kate left, they were making fishing plans for August. *August.* So now Mickey's a little in love with Leo too. They sit on the porch, and I cook and try not to eavesdrop until Kate calls and tells me to send him home. Leo wants to know about barbecuing ribs. Leo wants to know about solar panels. Mickey wants to know who in Hollywood Leo's seen naked.

Mickey tells Leo about the bird sanctuary, and he wants to check it out. Though I suggest it would be easier to drive there, we decide to make it our next morning run. I'm grateful for a new route and for the birds, and also for the fact that Leo comes on my runs now because it's another hour we're not apart.

If you're not going to drive, the only way into the bird sanctuary is through the forest on a rough path that runs parallel to a creek. The maple trees have sprouted fuzzy green flowers that dot the bright blue sky. Everything will look different in a month. I take this in quickly because I'm concentrating on the path ahead of me, strategically placing each foot to avoid the maze of aboveground roots at my feet. Parts of this run feel more like an obstacle course than a casual jog. We're sweating and we're laughing as each turn presents us with another fallen birch or muddy puddle to dodge. Leo calls over his shoulder that he kind of misses my Subaru, and I feel vindicated.

When the forest ends, I'm relieved. The path becomes wider, with seven-foot-tall wild pampas grass lining either side. The feathery tops bend with the breeze, directing us forward. I can no longer see the creek, but I can hear it as we run.

We disturb a family of turkeys, and when they run off, we see that we've arrived. We stop to catch our breath. We are in a meadow of yellow and lavender wildflowers with old oak and apple trees scattered among them. The creek has reappeared and winds its way through the meadow and beyond. We stay quiet to listen to the birds sing at one another across the trees. It's so orderly, in the back-and-forth rhythm of a conversation. I have never witnessed anything so beautiful.

"Well, this is new," I say.

"It is," he says and takes my sweaty hand.

"I mean, it's a nice change from my old loop."

"I mean, you're the first person I've ever been in love with," he says. Just like that. It's a Wednesday, I think, but I'm not even sure. In a meadow dotted with trees, covered in sweat with birds chirping around us, Leo Vance is in love with me. In that second, my life is like the tea house—I can see all the way through to the other side where there's an entirely different reality.

CHAPTER 13

❧

EVERYONE'S EXCITED AS WE PULL INTO THE DRIVEWAY after Thursday night's rehearsal. We are a week away from opening night, and with the exception of Frankie Bowfox stepping on Emma Schwab's dress and making her cry, it went off perfectly. Leo's ordered pizza, so the big metal box waits for us on the porch.

"There's a package here for you," I say, handing it to Leo.

"Me?" He brings the pizzas inside and tosses the package by the sink. "I'm starving."

"Do you need to open it?"

"Do you?" He smiles at me with a mouth full of pizza.

"Kinda," I shoot back. I open the envelope and pull out a script. *Mega Man*, it's called, and there's a Post-it note on the front: CALL ME IMMEDIATELY.

I hand it to him and he barely reacts, wiping tomato sauce off of Bernadette's cheek and then carefully rubbing it on the other one. There's a lot of laughing, and it's easy, and the future's rolling out in front of us perfectly.

I sometimes forget life's not a movie.

LEO'S ON THE phone in the tea house for a long time after dinner. The kids do their homework and linger. All of us know something's off. We busy ourselves with things so we can stay downstairs. I over-clean the kitchen, check and recheck the coffee maker. Arthur's running lines in a robot's voice. Bernadette colors in the cover of her notebook.

Leo is someone else when he walks through the back door. His shoes are wet from the lawn and he doesn't stop to take them off. As if trying to avoid the awful premonition I'm having, I focus on his shoes. They're black sneakers with a brown rubber sole. They're the same ones he always wears if he's not running or wearing flip-flops. I like this about Leo, the fact that as far as I know he only has three pairs of shoes. I like seeing them tucked under the daybed in the tea house. I need these shoes to stay.

"Hey, guys. Can we talk for a minute? I have some big news." He's all energy, pacing then sitting down and standing up. The three of us sit and wait; I can't think of any words. "So that was my agent, Jeremy. Paramount is going to do a big-budget action movie called *Mega Man*."

"I love Mega Man," says Arthur. *I hate Mega Man,* I think.

"Well, who doesn't?" He gives Arthur his biggest eyes.

"The director wants me for the role. I have to audition, but he's pretty sure I'm right for it."

I have words: "That's exciting. Right, guys?" I'm a mom again. He's leaving and I'm no longer a person who has sex all day. I'm neither beautiful nor compelling. I am Nora, and I am tumbling down a hill. Leo is going to "Asia," the mythical place where men go when they're tired of me. I need to grab my children and move them to safety before I roll into the abyss.

Bernadette's suspicious. "So what do you have to do?"

"The thing is they're on a tight schedule and need to get me approved right away." I almost jump in to explain how these things work, but I decide not to help him. He's going to have to say it himself. "I'm flying out to L.A. tomorrow morning."

So there it is. My heart is disintegrating into my intestines. I take a deep breath and look at my beautiful children. I cannot believe I've done this to them. I cannot believe I let them get in so deep with this guy, and he's leaving. We're 0 for 2.

Arthur shakes his head. "Leo, you can't go. The play's in a week. We haven't even done dress rehearsals."

Bernadette pipes up, "And I'm playing goalie Saturday against the Vipers." It's impossible to look away from the fact that my kids do not think of Leo as just a fun diversion, a houseguest who's helping with the play. They are counting on him.

Leo stops pacing. "I know, guys, and I can't believe I'm going to miss all that. But I'll be back by this time next week, for the last dress rehearsal and the big night. Mrs. Sasaki can totally handle it while I'm gone. Actually, you guys are so good you don't even need a director at this point. And, Bernie, I'll be here next weekend when you play Brookeville. You're going to kill it."

Arthur's quiet for a beat, as if deciding something. I wonder if he's comparing this moment to when Ben left. Ben said he'd be back in a vague way; he never gave an exact time. It's different, but there's a sameness too. Finally, he speaks. "Oh okay, that's cool. Well, good luck with the audition." He's trying not to cry, and he wants to leave with the upper hand. He offers Leo his hand to shake. "Thanks for all your help." Leo pulls him into a hug. Bernadette throws her arms around the two of them. She's crying.

Leo breaks the hugs and gets right in their faces. "You guys. Hear me. This is a week. And it's just how my work is. My plans get messed up."

Arthur takes in a deep breath. "Okay. A week." They all hug again, and I'm far away, watching this scene unfold.

"All right, you guys, it's late and tomorrow is huge!" I stretch out my arms to show just how huge tomorrow is and then hug them tight. "Run upstairs and brush teeth."

I haven't had a glass of wine and pouring one would give me something to do with my hands. I pull a bottle out of the fridge and start to open it. I need to find that thing that cuts the foil off. I think it's in the drawer with the carrot scraper but it's not. I am sure I used it yesterday so I look in the dishwasher, not that you'd ever wash that thing. The dishwasher is mercifully clean, so I start to unload it.

"Stop it," I hear. He's opening the bottle and pouring a glass. Just one.

"Thank you," I manage. My back is to the sink and I hold on to the cold porcelain.

"Listen, you have to understand how important this is to me. This is a huge movie, not a film. I think it's just the fun, family, normal thing I've been needing. It really feels right."

I notice he's holding my hand. And I think Ben did too, but I'm not sure. I thought we were just the fun, family, normal thing he needed. I thought this felt right. I suddenly remember what part of the movie we're in.

"How is this just a week? You need to film an entire movie." I don't know what I was thinking this whole time. How is he going to be a movie star while hanging out in my tea house all day?

"I'm going to go for the audition. Then, if it works out, I'll stay while they make a deal around the whole thing. Then I'll come back here until we start filming. And you can come with me. Or I'll come back on days off. Nora, I have a million ways to make this work. I have an airplane."

I want to be cool. I want to be the kind of person who can get through a week without Leo. I remember I used to be this person. I can barely remember her. I try to channel Naomi playing me while Ben is leaving.

"Okay. I'm excited for you. We'll figure it out. Have you packed everything?" My voice isn't right, but he's too revved up about this stupid movie to notice.

"There's not much, but my car's coming in twenty minutes so I should . . ." He pulls me into his arms and kisses me.

It's sweet and sad and I can't keep the tears from rolling down my face. "Hey, this isn't good-bye. I'll be back. Or you can come out. Whatever you want." He raises my chin so I'm forced to look at him. "It's just L.A."

And I don't know what that means. Does that mean I should be happy he's not disappearing into the ever-vague Asia? "It's just L.A.," I repeat back to him. And I like the sound of it. L.A. is a place you can come back from. I kiss him again and say, "Okay, go. I'm going up to the kids. Good luck."

Ten minutes later, there's a car in the driveway. Door open, door shut. It pulls away and I notice I've stopped reading *The Lightning Thief* out loud. Bernadette and Arthur are both in my bed, snuggled on each side. "It's okay to be sad, Mom. I'm sad," says Bernadette.

I squeeze her perfect little shoulder. "Thanks, Bernie. It'll be okay." I let them fall asleep in my bed because none of us is ready to be alone.

WHEN THE LIGHT starts to fill my room, I am already awake. I decide to skip the sunrise for the first time in forever and just lie in bed with my kids. The trickiest part of being a mom, especially a single mom, is knowing when it's okay to fall apart. Today they will wake up to a familiar feeling of loss, the light scab they've formed over the wound Ben left will be dislodged. I invited this in. Arthur will have to go to rehearsals and perform. I will too.

I stare at the cracked ceiling until I'm sure the sun's all the

NORA GOES OFF SCRIPT

way up. I wake my children with a hug. Bernadette wakes immediately and runs to get dressed. Arthur's not moving. "I think Fagin needs pancakes," I say, kissing his eyes awake.

"With chocolate chips," he mumbles.

I use up all of my adrenaline being chipper and getting them to school. Leo is in the air by now, but I check my phone for a text anyway. He'll be in L.A. by the time school's out, and I realize that will be the end of my knowing where he is. I grab my running shoes by the front door, and know I can't run. There is one single wineglass sitting on the counter, and I am stuck in time staring at it. I reach for my phone and text Kate: Come over.

She finds me still standing in the kitchen. "What happened? Where is he?"

"He's gone. L.A. Big movie." And I start to cry. Kate moves me to the couch, and I am so grateful to give in to it. Between sobs, I give details, and she is patient with me.

When I've cried myself out, she says, "Okay. You've got to bear with me. This is really uncharted territory. I've never seen you cry before. Like even last time when your actual husband left."

I nod. "That was different. Like, why would I want him around if he didn't want to be here. But this." I start to cry again. "I still want him here."

"He's only been gone twelve hours, and he says he's coming back."

"Do you really think he is?" I'm mopping my face with my sleeve and clinging to her words.

"Why would he say he's coming back if he didn't mean it?

137

He's going to be back a week from yesterday. That's not even a week."

"It's too long," I say, slumping into her lap.

IT'S SATURDAY, AND Bernadette stops six goals against the Vipers. It's a big deal if you're eight years old, but instead of "Congratulations," all anyone says to us is, "Where's Leo?" It's the only thing people can think of to say to me. "Where's Leo?" is practically a greeting. I say the words "L.A.," "audition," "Thursday" so many times that it becomes a tune that I sing as I move through the crowd. When we're finally at my car and I've loaded my single chair into the trunk, I text Leo a video clip of Bernadette winning the game with a diving catch.

He responds immediately, and my heart rate quickens: I can't believe I missed that. Give her a hug from me.

Me: She's so happy

Leo: What's next?

Me: Quick lunch, lightbulbs, and then Little League

Leo: Ugh. Good luck. Love you.

"WHERE'S LEO?" MR. Mapleton greets us as we walk into his store.

"L.A. An audition," I say again.

"He's coming back," says Bernadette.

"Did he give a specific day?" he asks. He's stopped sorting

NORA GOES OFF SCRIPT

through the pile of drill bits on the counter. I have his full attention.

"Thursday," I say.

Mr. Mapleton smiles. "Ah, then he's coming back. As long as he has a plane ticket for a specific day, he'll be back. Good," he says, reassuring himself.

Leo doesn't buy plane tickets, I don't say. "Arthur's play is Friday night. That's more solid than a plane ticket," I say. I am promising things over which I have no control, but I've succeeded in saying the words that will soothe me and keep Mr. Mapleton from feeling sorry for me. Arthur squeezes my hand, making me feel like maybe I've soothed him too.

Arthur actually has a pretty good game. He has a base hit and no errors. I want to text Leo about this, but sort of feel like it's too much. I'll tell him when he reaches out to me. That's what a normal, not obsessed, girlfriend would do. And for now, that's what I'll pretend to be. He's doing his thing and has other stuff on his mind, I'll pretend I do too.

THERE'S SOMETHING GOING on with the director. Leo's telling me about it on the phone Tuesday night. I'm lying in bed and he's saying a lot of words. I just like hearing the sound of his voice.

"I mean, I would have wanted the part without Bohai directing," he's saying. "But the chance to work with him sort of clinched it. If they fire him, it'll be a lot of starting over again."

"And why would they fire him again?" I'm getting sleepy. I want him to keep talking.

"If these accusations have any truth to them, then he's a creep and no one's going to want to work with him, including me. I was supposed to have dinner tonight with the producer to find out more, but she canceled."

"What are you doing for dinner then?"

"I bought a chicken, actually." Leo sounds truly pleased with himself. "And a salad."

"Wait. You're cooking?"

"No. Well, I thought about it. I went to Whole Foods. Have you ever been to a Whole Foods?"

"I have."

"It's nicer than the Stop n' Save."

"It is."

"Well, they have a lot of chicken. I just stood there looking at all the raw chickens and kind of freaked out. Two people stopped and took my picture while I was studying them. I didn't think I could figure it out without you, but did you know they sell chickens already cooked? And salad?"

I laugh. "Yes, I did know this. Listen, when you come back, I'll walk you through roasting a chicken."

Leo's quiet for a second. "No, thanks. I just want you to roast me a chicken. I don't ever want to eat another chicken that wasn't roasted by you."

My desire to put on an apron and roast this man a chicken is profound. I don't even own an apron. I just want him to be close enough to me that I can hand him a plate with chicken on it. "Okay," I say. "Let tonight be the last non-Nora chicken you ever eat."

I CAN'T WAIT to talk to him on Wednesday night, because I'm going to get to say, "See you tomorrow!" Bernadette and Arthur are unusually upbeat at dinner for the same reason. They brush their teeth and move their bathroom stuff into mine, in preparation.

Around nine o'clock I get a text from Leo: It's all hitting the fan. Just google "Bohai" and you'll see. The studio's fired him and I need to meet the new director tonight. Good chance I'm not going to get there till Friday. I'll text you after dinner? Or should I let you sleep?

I say: That's okay, text me.

And I mean that it's okay to wake me up because I'd rather talk to him than sleep. I do not mean that not coming until Friday is okay. I wake to the sunrise and two texts from Leo. They came in at two o'clock and hadn't woken me.

Leo: Hey. Too late to call?

Ten minutes later: Glad you're getting some sleep. Tonight was a lot, I actually like the new guy but there are going to be tons of changes. There's no way I get there before Friday. So sorry. Love you.

So it's not today. I'll wait another day. What's the big deal? I tell the kids at breakfast. "So Leo texted me in the middle of the night. They had to hire a new director so he can't come till Friday."

"I got the same text," says Arthur to his eggs.

"See," says Bernadette. "This is why I need a cell phone.

It's not fair that Leo texts you guys and not me. I'm totally left out of this family." That last word gives me pause.

"You're eight," I say. "If I bought an eight-year-old a cell phone so she could text with a movie star, I'm pretty sure they'd run me out of Laurel Ridge." I smile at her and get a glare in return.

"You think he'll come Friday?" Arthur asks. I can tell he's nervous to ask it.

"Of course! It's the play. Leo's living for this." My voice has gone high-pitched, like I'm selling something. Arthur gives me a pinched smile. The truth is that I have no business making promises about a school play on behalf of a man who's working on a film with a 250-million-dollar budget. Leo has reentered something that is bigger than we are. I've lost my chance to manage Arthur's expectations, mainly because I don't want to look at the possibility that Leo will break both of our hearts.

I don't hear from Leo all day Thursday. I assume whatever is keeping him in L.A. is keeping him busy. He's working with the new director. There was something about getting fitted for a slightly different costume situation. I know he's busy, but when he hasn't called by dinnertime to say those three little words, "See you tomorrow!" I feel kind of sick. My own selfish heart needs him back. More than that, I cannot bear the thought of his disappointing Arthur.

I wake Friday morning to see he texted during the night: I'm really sorry, there's no way out of here. If I leave the whole project falls apart. I'm not sure when I can get back. I'll call you when I can.

I feel like I've been punched in the gut. Besides the pain

of it, my overwhelming feeling is that I should not have let myself get punched in the gut. I have let down my guard in the most epic way. Arthur is going to be devastated. Frankly, the whole town is. The thought of walking into that auditorium tonight to a chorus of "Where's Leo?" makes me want to scream.

Arthur finds me on the porch with my coffee. "I got the text too," he says. "This sucks."

"It does," I say and put my arm around him. "It really does. But you are going to be so great tonight, and the whole town is coming to cheer you on."

"We don't need him." He looks at me hard, studying my face. "Are you okay?"

"Of course," I say, and we both know I'm lying.

"Your eyes look like you were crying," he says.

"Allergies," I say.

He scoots closer to me and takes my hand in his. "Please be okay, Mom." And I know what he means: I'm all he has.

WE ARE THIRTY minutes till curtain and I am scanning the crowd, because deep down, I am still a romance writer. I know this scene, I've written it thirty-four times. The commercial break is over. This is the community event, and just after it's gotten started and the heroine has moved on and found a way to manage alone, he appears as if by magic. He's had an epiphany and this is the life he wants. Chaste kiss and on with the town fair, soup kitchen opening, ballet performance. Fifth-grade play.

Kate's covering for me backstage so Bernadette and I can sit in the third row and watch. Mrs. Sasaki seems thrilled to take the credit for Leo's directorial debut. Oliver is good. Fagin is great. I'm grateful for the dark when he sings "You can go but be back soon . . ." because there are tears. Bernadette takes my hand.

In the end there are standing ovations. Arthur smiles from the inside, a smile that tells me that he knows who he is and he knows he can do things. The basic truth of parenting fills my heart: If your kids are okay, you don't really have any problems. I will relish this feeling. I will keep squeezing Bernadette's hand.

IT'S FRIDAY NIGHT so there's no homework and no rush to bed. It's cool enough to light a fire and we squeeze together on the sunroom couch. We haven't sat out here in a while, because there would have been no room for Leo. Now that he's gone, everything feels sort of empty, so we gravitate toward the smaller space. We review the performance as if we are unbiased and conclude that Fagin stole the show. They are so tentative with me that I realize I need to say something about Leo to break the tension.

"I bet Leo's really sorry he missed tonight. He worked almost as hard as you did." It's an opening.

"I'm sure he's fine," Arthur says. "He can order the DVD." This might take a while.

When I get into bed, my phone dings. Leo: How'd it go?

Me: He was fantastic, stole the show. How's it going there?

Leo: It's chaos, but we're making progress. I think it's going to be a good movie.

I lie: That's great! So happy for you!

Leo: Thanks. I have to head out to dinner. But I love you and I really miss you.

Me: Love you too.

I am awash with relief. He's coming back; he loves me. I don't need to act like such a baby. "My boyfriend is away for work," I say out loud. And I like the sound of it. I mean, I lived with a man who refused to work for a decade, and now I'm complaining that the new guy works too much? Come on. Leo's work is a huge part of who he is, and that's going to be part of our relationship. I decide that "relationship" is a nice word, and I fall asleep.

I don't hear from him on Saturday. Like the whole day, no call and no text. I reassure myself by rereading the transcript. He loves me, he misses me. I don't hear from him on Sunday. It's the weekend, I tell myself. Maybe people in L.A. work on the weekend. It occurs to me that I can text him.

Me: Hey

No reply. I stare at my phone and try to come up with the reasons he might not be responding. Well, maybe they've started filming already and he's on set. Maybe he's out to brunch with his agent. Maybe he's swimming laps in his giant pool. With deep breaths, I remind myself I'm not in middle school.

CHAPTER 14

ﾐﾐﾐﾐﾐ

O N MONDAY, I GO FOR A RUN WITHOUT MY PHONE,
sure that if I leave it in the kitchen, I will return to
multiple missed calls from Leo. A watched pot and
all that. I finish my run in record time and am surprised,
maybe gobsmacked, to find that I'd missed nothing at all.

By Monday night, the feel of my un-ringing phone in my
hand is torture. My new plan is to leave the phone in the sunroom so that I can be present with my kids for homework,
dinner, *Wheel of Fortune*. By removing my attention, I will
trick my phone into ringing.

I check it before I take my kids upstairs. Nothing. I pun-
ish my phone by leaving it in the sunroom while we read. It
punishes me back by not ringing. I take it with me out onto
the porch to watch the blackness of the night, and I feel
uniquely powerless, as if the entirety of my happiness lies in
someone else's hands. I don't know where I lost my power. He

wanted to stay. He kissed me. He said he loved me. How am I suddenly Elizabeth Bennet, wandering the moors and hoping Mr. Darcy shows up?

This last thought annoys my sensibilities enough that my fingers dial Leo's number. My throat is tight as the call connects and I hear the first ring. He's going to say "hey" and explain where he's been. I'm going to act cool about it. Second ring, third ring. My heart sinks when the call goes to voicemail. I listen all the way to the end, just to hear his voice, before I hang up.

He'll see that I called and call me back when he's free. I go to bed with the ringer on high volume so I won't miss it.

ON TUESDAY, I text Kate to tell her he's not coming back. She's at my door in ten minutes.

I'm not crying when I open the door. "Let's quit the usual crap about how maybe he lost his phone or is stuck under a bus. There's no reality where it's normal that a person who texts me three hours a night after spending the entire day with me just stops. Unless he's decided to. And if he was dead, it would be in the news."

"Are you done?" She pushes past me and puts a box of cookies on the counter.

"Probably not." I pour some coffee for each of us and take a cookie. "I just need you to be sensible and honest with me. I feel like I can't trust my own mind right now. 'I love you. I miss you' and poof? At least Ben was honest enough to tell me."

NORA GOES OFF SCRIPT

"Okay, so now Ben's the model for male behavior?" We're sitting at my kitchen counter, side by side, mugs in hand.

"Tell me what to think," I say.

"I agree it's weird. I'd be less surprised if it sort of dwindled away. Like fewer, shorter texts. 'I love you' turns to 'love you' turns to 'ly.' That kind of thing."

"That's actually what I thought would happen. The slow exit. Not like immediate out of sight, out of mind. And he's in freakin' L.A., where women have actual suntans and highlights. Staring at that all day, it's hard to remember why you were in love with the woman with the unruly hair and flowy tops."

"I've been meaning to talk to you about that," she kids.

A car pulls up and my heart is in my throat. He's changed his mind. He's returning my text in person to tell me he's going to stay and direct children's theater full-time. "Go see what it is," I tell her, head in hands.

It's a courier, asking Kate to sign for an envelope with my name on it. It's too thick to be a love letter, and I hate myself for living in one of my own screenplays. No one writes love letters and has them hand delivered. I open it and find a stack of hundred-dollar bills and a note from Weezie: *Hey, Nora, Leo says he owes you back rent. Thanks again for taking care of him. Here's hoping L.A. works out! Weezie.*

I count out twenty-one thousand dollars. "Oh my God. I'm being paid off." I start to cry, but then I'm so mad that my tears dry up. I explain to Kate how we agreed on seven thousand dollars for seven days. But when he decided to stay and help Arthur, I had no intention of charging him. I was sleeping with him for God's sake. What did that even make this?

I grab my phone and Kate stops me. "Wait. Let's rehearse before you go off half-cocked."

"I'm just texting Weezie," I say. But my heart is beating so fast that I can't type. "You do it." I hand her my phone and dictate: "Hey, Weezie! Hope you're good! Thanks for the cash, but that was way too much. I was only charging him for the first seven days, so I'll have the rest dropped back to you. Please send address? Thanks!"

Kate shows me the text to review. "That's way too many exclamation points. I look like a maniac." She deletes one, then two, and finally we think we've struck the right mood and she sends.

Immediately typing bubbles appear. Oh, wow. I must have misunderstood his text. Okay, thanks! I'm shacked up at his place for I don't know how long. Next text is his address, a penthouse on Sixty-Fifth Street.

"Well done. She's matched you in exclamation points. Now we need to get your shit together." Kate urges me toward the shower and goes out to inspect the tea house. She returns with two empty wineglasses and all of his bedding. I come downstairs towel drying my hair and find her fondling his sheets.

"So what did you want me to do with these? Any chance I can keep them?"

"Take them directly to your car."

One time in high school my boyfriend dumped me and

my best friend Ellen and I ate ice cream until we were sick. I made out with this guy freshman year in college, and when he never called me, my roommate and I got drunk. As I look at Kate now, I can't think of any self-destructive pastime that will make me feel better. I'm aware that I am going to need all of my reserves to get through this.

"What are you going to tell the kids?"

"They know." As I say it, I realize that it's true. They haven't mentioned his name in days. They're careful around me, overly thoughtful. Wasn't I the one who was supposed to be protecting them from another broken heart? "Maybe they just assumed. It's Ben all over again."

ON WEDNESDAY MORNING I drop the kids at school, force myself to run, and then somehow find myself in the car headed south on I-95 toward the city. My intention is benign; I need to return the money that does not belong to me. And in returning that money, I will set off a chain of events wherein Weezie as his proxy will have to inform him that the money has been returned, triggering the memory of me in Leo's mind. He will have no choice but to stop what he is doing and call me. Nora, he'll say, I miss you so much, and your returning this money shows me just what a good and true person you are. I'll be on the next flight . . .

Oh, also, I've gone completely insane. My second reason for delivering this money is that I definitely need a change of scenery. And by "change of scenery" I mean I need to see where he lives. Somehow this will help, I tell myself, coming to see his city life so that I can release him to it. Yes, this is a great idea.

I get off the FDR on Sixty-Third Street and head west. I find a parking garage on Sixty-Fifth and Lexington Avenue and decide to stop there so I can enter his neighborhood on foot. As I walk west the streets become less congested, though it always feels like it's garbage day in Manhattan. I cross Park Avenue and look both ways, up and down the median. They've planted tulips in red and yellow, and I stop to take a photo.

Women pass me in heels I could never stand in. I look down at my peasant top, jeans, and sandals and think, *When did I turn into Carole King?* His apartment is between Madison and Fifth Avenues. The town houses that line both sides of the street are exquisite brick and limestone buildings, and I have a momentary feeling that I am trespassing. His is a pre-war doorman building in the middle of the block. I loiter and wonder not for the first time how I got here.

I'm walking into the building through the narrow, gilded door and the doorman stands to greet me. "May I help you, ma'am?"

"Yes, I have something for Leo. Vance." I indicate the envelope but don't offer it to him. I realize that I'm not ready to leave. "Is Weezie here?"

"I believe so. May I have your name?"

"Nora. Nora Hamilton." He dials and I am full of regret. I don't have anything to say to Weezie, and there's no reason for her to know I drove ninety minutes to see Leo's apartment.

"She says to go right up. Just press PH in the elevator on the left."

I'm grateful it's not one of those elevators where the doorman has to ride with you to operate the thing. I press PH and take advantage of the mirrored wall and long ride to check my teeth and my overall bearing. Teeth are fine, but I've lost weight in just three days, and I look really tired.

The door opens into a small foyer with a marble table and an umbrella stand. There's only one door to knock on and it's already open. "Nora! This is so fun! What are you doing here?" Weezie is in her pajamas and has a bagel in her hand. "Come in. Come in."

"I'm really sorry to drop in like this, but I had an appointment in the city so I thought I'd drop off the money in person." Everything is marble and cream. Couches and chairs are arranged so that conversations won't last more than twenty minutes. There is no place to get cozy. I scan the space for a personal photograph. This place belongs to no one.

"What kind of appointment?" she's asking me.

"Hair," I say too quickly and now she's looking at mine, which has certainly not just stepped out of the salon. "I mean I'm going to an appointment. Gotta do something about this hair, right?"

"I think you look great. Kinda Carole King." Oh my God. "It must feel so good to have your house back to yourself, especially after a surprise houseguest." Weezie rolls her eyes and motions me into the kitchen. "Coffee?"

"Sure," I say, because I want to see his coffee mugs. She

hands me a white mug that's straight out of a hotel restaurant. "This place is really stark. Does Leo spend a lot of time here?"

"Ha. He hates it too. Naomi's decorator did the whole thing while they were in Saint Bart's in January. He said 'surprise me!' and she really did. Naomi loved it but Leo kept saying he didn't know where to sit. Still doesn't."

"I don't understand," is all I can say.

"He just didn't grow up like this; he likes things a little more homey."

"No, I mean about Naomi. Why were they away together? Filming?"

"No, being madly in love. That's Leo for you. He falls hard, and then he's out just as fast. Naomi was actually an exception because she dumped him. I'm sure he told you. Third day of *The Tea House* shoot."

"I see," I say, because I do. I really do. "That explains why he was kind of a drunk mess during the rest of the filming." I give a little laugh to show that I find this sort of juvenile behavior amusing.

"Well, he owes you a lot. Seems like a little quiet time in the country screwed his head on straight, and now he's starring in the highest budget film of his lifetime."

"Is it still on?"

"Yeah, I should have said. They start filming week after next."

I've got to get myself out of this room. I chug my coffee, which is hot and burns my throat, and say, "Well, good luck to both of you. I've got to get this hair taken care of, a little less Carole King and little more Naomi Sanchez, if you know

NORA GOES OFF SCRIPT

what I mean." I am talking too fast and being too glib. I grab my bag and give her a quick hug. "Take care."

"Oh no," Weezie says, and I stop. "You're in love with him."

I'm a pretty good liar. I can fake my way through a lot of uncomfortable social situations. Heck, my sister's a New York socialite. I've faked my way through dinners with her friends where they complain about how their nannies insist on getting paid on holidays. But in this moment, I cannot muster, "Oh, don't be ridiculous." I'm so raw, and the thought of spilling it to someone who might have some insight is irresistible.

"I am."

"Oh no," she says again. "Did you . . . ?"

"Yes. And he told me he loves me, about a thousand times. I can prove it," I say, holding my phone up. "He couldn't go two hours without seeing me, touching me, texting me from a hundred yards away. And now I haven't heard from him since Friday."

Weezie looks crestfallen. "I'm really sorry. That's not his usual MO, at least not as far as I know. None of them ever told me he'd said he loved them." None of them.

"So he's not in jail or lost his phone or in the hospital with amnesia," I offer.

"Nope. There's got to be something really weird going on here if he's ghosting you."

I hug Weezie because I'm supremely grateful that she's been honest with me. The last thing I need is someone feeding me false hope through a morphine drip. I need to face the very simple facts here and move on.

The elevator is waiting for me, thank God. Better still, there are sunglasses in my purse. I smile to the doorman and head out into midday sun. I am a fool. It's all so clear to me now that I don't know how I twisted my mind to avoid it. I must have been having a post-divorce psychotic break. I've let myself slip into one of my idiotic fantasy stories.

Facts: Leo was sleeping with Naomi Sanchez. Men who sleep with women like Naomi Sanchez don't fall in love with women like me. I was a woman with a welcoming, homey house. I was a place where he stopped for a while to recover. He's had four days to call and he hasn't. He used money to assuage his guilt. I was a place to rest so that he would be in the right state of mind to rise up and score the biggest movie of his career. I suddenly regret returning the money.

CHAPTER 15

❧

I SPEND THE WEEK TRYING TO RECLAIM MY HOUSE. I START with the sunrise, which I try to enjoy but mostly cry through. I find bright green bedding for the tea house and force myself to sit at the table for an hour a day. I don't write. How did I let this man stop by for three weeks and steal my heart, my house, and my career?

Sometimes I can't breathe. Like I walk into a space we once shared and the sound of his voice arrests me. I can hear his voice saying something that must not be true. I'll just stand there, struck by the pain of it. My mind chases its tail— he said he loved me and he was coming back and he's not calling and he had a third party send cash but he said he loved me and he was coming back.

School pickup is a slow death, thirty minutes at a time. I try to arrive a little bit late so I don't have to say these things:

Yes, it's exciting about the movie. No, I haven't heard from him. I'm fine, really.

Kate moves me around like she's my handler, throwing her body between me and any particularly offensive comments. I'm raw and exposed. I understand what that means now; I feel like I don't have skin. I should never have been out with him in public. I could have kept this to myself. I didn't need to kiss him at two P.M. in the middle of town.

People felt bad for me when Ben left, but no one really liked him. No one really thought I was happy either. To have seen me with Leo, probably grinning like a lovesick kid, they must have seen this coming. *Leo Vance isn't going to stay in Laurel Ridge with that woman forever. She's setting herself up for a fall.* Real or imagined, *We knew it!* is what I see on their faces. Everyone but me saw this coming.

I don't know where Kate is when I find myself on the receiving end of Vicky Miller's pouty face. I have to give Ben credit, she really is a very attractive woman. Blond and fit and nicely maintained. "I heard," she says.

"Oh," I say, looking over her shoulder for a way out. She's stepping closer to me and to my horror her arms are reaching out to pull me into a hug. The thought of it is unbearable. "Wait. You're not going to touch me, are you?"

"Of course. I just want to give you a hug. I feel terrible."

"Because you slept with my husband? Or about Leo?" That's how raw I am. I don't care who on the playground knows. I don't care if I seem a little crazy. All I know is that if this woman touches me with her self-pity, I will die.

NORA GOES OFF SCRIPT

"Nora," Vicky says in the most maddening way, a cousin of "calm down."

Kate swoops in from wherever she's been slacking off and links her arm in mine to drag me away. "She knows," she says to Vicky over her shoulder. "Everyone knows, and we think you're gross."

This makes me smile as she maneuvers me to the other end of the blacktop. "Gross?" I say. "That's like the kid in school who eats his boogers."

"Give me a break," she says. "I'm new to this."

"You're a good egg," I say.

"I have to tell you something," she says. And she's nervous.

"Tell me you're pregnant," I say.

"No. I've been paid off too. By Leo."

It's really hot on the blacktop and I am feeling hazy. "What are you talking about?"

"I got a check today for Ready Set for a hundred thousand dollars from Leo Vance's Charitable Trust." She gives me a second to hear it. "And I know he's the devil and he uses money to ease his guilt for being a total creep, but that money could help me double the reach of my program over the next two years. Like, it could change everything."

"What is wrong with him?" I say, repeating my favorite rhetorical question.

"So you want me to return it?" Kate looks like she's about to start begging.

"Sorry. No, of course not. Keep the money, that's amazing. I just don't know how a guy who has the time to call his charitable trust and initiate a donation doesn't have time to return my text and say, 'Hey sorry, I'm out.'"

"At least he feels guilty; like, at least he knows he's a jerk," she says.

"I don't know. I didn't think I could feel worse. But Leo feeling sorry for me is sort of next-level bad."

WHEN SCHOOL'S OUT in June, I decide to take my kids up to my parents' house in the Adirondacks for two weeks. When my parents moved out of Chesterville and my dad sold his pool-cleaning business, he insisted they retire on a lake. All that water to swim in, he said to anyone who would listen, and no one has to clean it.

I've paid this month's mortgage and taxes, my credit cards are paid off, and I have $8,329 in the bank. I am not ready to go back into the tea house to write. Maybe I'll be able to write something someplace else. I also hope that with my parents as a distraction for my kids, I might be able to fall apart a little.

My parents make everything seem easy. My mom told me once, "The secret to a happy marriage is that you give a hundred and ten percent to him and he gives a hundred and ten percent to you." In spite of the maddening mathematical impossibility of this statement, I always liked the sound of it. My parents are like a couple of cartoon magpies, always offering themselves up to each other. They were high school sweethearts, and she worked as a nanny while he started his pool-cleaning business. Everything he has, he credits to her. And vice versa.

160

It's possible that growing up watching the fantasy of this marriage is what makes writing romance movies so easy. My parents make me believe that some people really are made for each other and that a joyful, easy marriage is possible. Two people who love each other and are looking in the same direction can build a wonderful life. I've caught myself using my parents' gestures and quirks in movies, making me wonder if they're the prototype couple I keep tweaking over and over again.

Penny and Rick have their own high-powered version of this partnership, though I've never really witnessed the joy in it. They both give a hundred and ten percent, and they're focused on the same things. They just don't seem all that focused on each other. I got marriage half right. I gave a hundred and ten percent and Ben gave nothing, leaving us at an average of just fifty-five percent, which is a fail in pretty much anyone's book.

At the cabin, my dad takes my kids out in the boat every morning to water-ski and ride inner tubes. Arthur doesn't leave my dad's side, like he thinks he's the last man in the world. Which he may be.

In the afternoons we play cards and nap and talk about dinner. I take walks and cry, but it's less raw here. It's actually a Leo-free zone. No one mentions him, and I don't have to walk through the room where he kissed me for the first time. I don't have to see the pity in Mr. Mapleton's eyes every time I need vacuum cleaner bags.

Or the rage in Mickey's. Mickey has taken this whole thing personally, like he himself was seduced by Leo and then abandoned. "He said he was staying," he says, incredulous. "He was going to buy the Big Green Egg and we were going to cook ribs." Those ribs were Mickey's forever. I totally get it. We were all duped.

Mom and I are in the kitchen cleaning up the dinner dishes, while my dad and the kids take their food comas to the TV room. "You're awfully thin," she starts.

"Am I?"

"It's not a happy thin either. What's going on?"

"Nothing. The same. Maybe running too much."

"No word from Ben?"

"He's not coming back, Mom."

"What an asshole," she says, and we both laugh. My mom saves her swears for special occasions.

"I don't miss him," I say. "I'm really much happier without him."

"That's good. And all the excitement with the movie and that movie star staying with you, that must have been a real pick-me-up."

"Yeah, it was something."

"Mom! It's Leo!" Bernadette screams from the TV room, and I drop the glass I'm drying.

Mom and I run over, and there he is on *TMZ*, walking out of a club with Naomi, his arm around her shoulders. I can't look away, but I can feel my mom watching me. "Oh dear," she says.

The next day she wants to hike. "Tell me," she says before we're even out of the driveway.

"Long version or short version?"

"I've got all the time in the world," she says.

"I think I only have the energy for the short version. We had this big romance, like really big. He got called away to film a movie, and I haven't heard from him since. And clearly, he's not dead."

"That sounds like some kind of a fantasy, like something Penny would have cooked up."

"If you're trying to say it doesn't sound like me, I couldn't agree more. It's like I suffered temporary insanity."

"Sometimes that's what love is," she says.

PENNY ARRIVES THE next day with her family, and as I watch them file out of her square of a Mercedes G-Wagon, two adults followed by two matching children, another square, I am acutely aware that my family is a triangle.

My kids appear out of nowhere and throw themselves into the twins. Ethan and Maxwell are nine and slide in perfectly between Arthur and Bernadette. Whenever he's with his cousins, Arthur becomes almost manly. He concocts feats of strength as games, and I suspect it's because they're the only kids he's ever known who are less athletic than he. As a result, Penny thinks Arthur's kind of rough, which cracks me up.

"Hey, Pen. Hey, Rick," I say, hugging them both. Penny holds me for an extra few beats to convey her love and support and sympathy for how pathetic my life is. I am grateful to receive the sentiment without having to hear the words. Rick points to his AirPods indicating that he's on a call. Rick's pretty much always on a call.

"You're thin," Penny says, putting her arm around me and leading me away from Rick.

"I've heard."

"So no word?"

"Not a one," I say.

"If you want, you can let this go," she says. "Because I hate him enough for both of us." Penny is fierce, and my whole life I have loved having her on my side. I want to borrow her hatred and inject it into my heart. Anger would feel better than what I'm feeling.

The kids are all going to bunk up in the loft, and they've run up there to negotiate beds. I grab some beers and we settle in on the deck, watching the boats go by. Just two summers ago, during this week, Ben was with us. My family was a square too. He was slightly hostile to Rick the whole time, for no reason that I could discern, except for the fact that Rick is rich and pays when we go out to dinner. That's actually my favorite thing about Rick.

Penny's initial enthusiasm about Ben and his family faded as she got to know him. Ben was never shy about belittling my work in front of other people, almost as if he was hoping to build a consensus about how pointless it was. She and Rick got excited hearing about his first couple of business ventures, but then just got sort of quiet over the next dozen. The last time the four of us had dinner, Ben droned on about an app he was going to develop with a Chinese guy he met online. "You're sure lucky you have Nora," Rick said as he signed the check.

Besides that moment, I've never really liked Rick, or more

accurately, I've never been able to see his humanity. Like he's formal with his kids, polite to my parents and me. He treats Penny like a business partner, like they're board members of their family unit. While this part of their marriage doesn't exactly sweep this romance writer off her feet, I know that at the core of their marriage is an unshakable mutual respect. No eye rolling, no sarcasm. Still, I've always had the feeling I'd like Rick more if I saw him cry or throw up.

Rick finishes sending an email and surveys us all, as if remembering where he is. "So, Nora, how's Hollywood treating you? Big time, right?"

"Yeah, well we'll see. The movie comes out in October; I hope people like it."

"So'd you get a two-movie deal or anything? What's next?"

"Nope. But I was thinking about a second beer," I say, looking to my mom to change the subject.

Penny gets excited. "You know what you should do now?" Oh brother. "You should write an epically romantic, big-screen love story. Like a fantasy romance, with scenes like those two paddling through the rain in *The Notebook*. Like the kind we'd cry all the way through."

"I'm not sure I'm cut out for that," I say.

"Just think of the most romantic moment of your life and build a story around it. This is what you do. It doesn't need to be formulaic, just make it real."

There's something about Penny's use of the word "just" that always reminds me how much easier her life is than mine. It's not only her money and her supportive husband. Penny is prone to doing without overthinking. Just hire a cleaning lady. Just meet someone else. Just whip up another movie. But in this instance, she's onto something. I can feel it tingling on the top of my head. What if I could write the story of Leo and me? What if by writing it, I could be rid of it, stop ruminating on it? What if I could write my way out of this hole?

AFTER THE FOURTH of July we are back in Laurel Ridge and settled into the slow soupy routine of summer. Arthur has turned eleven and is sleeping later, leaving Bernadette and me to our morning routines. Bernadette has an all-day soccer camp that starts at nine. Arthur has an acting camp that starts at noon. I have time for my run between drop-offs, but there is no real time to settle in and write.

I decide not to fight the situation, to give myself a real summer vacation from work. I'll be broke by the end of September, and I'll probably have to run up a little debt before I sell another TRC movie. The thought of going back into any debt at all makes me feel like my hair has been set on fire, but the thought of going back into the tea house is worse.

Even just standing at the sunroom window and seeing those gorgeous hydrangea at either side of the tea house door, the ones that Leo is not, in fact, here in July to see, is too much for me. It's ridiculous but I look at them and see a lie: He did not wait around to see what would bloom in July; he did not stay. Bernadette likes to cut them and bring them into the house, which is normally the joy of our summer, open windows and giant blue hydrangea covering every surface. This year I suggest she put them all in her room.

I consider trying to write at the library, but the truth is I'm not ready to write at all. I'm not ready to make light of love affairs and heartbreak. I certainly can't see myself moving toward a happy ending. I know that I need to build my world back up around me. My schedule was my armor and I need to reconstruct it. I need new routines so that I don't see Leo every time I roast a chicken. Plenty of people don't roast chickens, and I will be one of them.

I'm not entirely focused on self-improvement. During the quiet hours when both of my kids are gone, I curl up on the couch and watch Dr. Phil or reality shows about people who have it worse than me. The idea here, I tell myself, is that it will help me feel better about my life. At least I didn't send my life savings to a fake online boyfriend. At least I don't have a compulsion to eat my own hair. In the end, I don't feel better about my life. I just feel depressed that these people have it so bad.

At night I get in bed and scroll through his Instagram account. I know he doesn't post his own stuff; I don't even think he has Instagram on his phone. But whoever his agent hired to entertain Leo's thirty million followers has to be getting his photos from somewhere. There are photos from the set of *Mega Man*, a few from around his house in L.A. *Leo's hair is longer. Leo's wearing pastels now.* There's a happy birthday post to Naomi, a candid shot of the two of them on the set of *The Tea House*. I zoom in on Leo for clues as to who he is. One of these nights there will be a photo of him that reveals a trace of malice or, better, heartache on his face, and it will all make sense to me.

There's one photo of the sunset that I swear he didn't take. I don't know how I know this, but I just know it isn't how he would have captured it. This thought sets me back. It bothers me that I knew him so well. It bothers me that I can jump right back into his head and know what he'd think, when I actually have no idea who he is now. *Maybe he did take that photo,* I think. *Maybe that's how he sees things now.* I vow to delete Instagram from my phone in the morning. I don't delete Instagram.

My kids and I are careful with one another. They don't know how to talk about this situation with Leo, and I suspect it's because they don't know what it was. All they know is that everything feels different without him, especially me. I try to bring Leo up in passing to keep him from being such a loaded topic. I try to talk about him as a thing that happened, a little excitement, but not a thing that we are bringing into the future.

Arthur's camp is putting on a production of *West Side Story* to be performed for the whole town in mid-August. He can't stand the director. "It's like he doesn't know anything about acting. He's a gym teacher the rest of the year. All he ever does is tell us where to stand." The main problem with this guy, I suspect, is that he's not Leo.

I decide to take the opening. "That's disappointing. But it

was pretty unusual that you had a real movie star directing your last play."

"I guess." Arthur looks out the car window.

I try again. "Good thing you didn't promise Leo you'd never pursue acting. Seems like it's starting to be your thing."

"Yeah, like Leo's so big on promises."

CHAPTER 16

I T'S SEPTEMBER, AND I'M BACK. THIS IS WHAT I TELL MYSELF. I'd allotted myself a lazy period of mourning, and now it's over. I am almost completely out of money so, effectively, I have constructed a situation where I will be forced to write to survive. I even spent two hundred dollars I probably shouldn't have hosting a big Labor Day barbecue in the backyard. It was worth it. I set up the bar on the table in the tea house, and people wandered in and out, cleansing it. Someone spilled a margarita on the floor, and I almost said, *Thank you.* The best antidote to old memories is new ones.

At sunrise on the first day of school, I vow to stay snapped out of it. Today I will return to my pre–*The Tea House* self, and I will write. I'm a little tan; I'm my normal weight. I'm even doing some of the runs Leo and I did together, though I haven't been to the bird sanctuary. I'm not insane.

When I walk out to the tea house, the door is closed. This

has to work today, so I open the door, just the way I like it, and go back into my house to start again. I make a fresh mug of tea and re-sharpen my pencils. I approach the tea house and that old feeling is there. It's a combination of inspiration and motivation. It's magic, and I'm about to enter another world. I set my things down just so and build the fire.

Hair in a knot, I open my laptop and begin to type. I promised Jackie I'd have a complete script for TRC by October 1, which really shouldn't be a problem. I write the story of a male actor from Manhattan who goes out to an old country house to film a movie and falls in love with the woman who lives there. They butt heads for a while, but then he steps in and helps with the school play. On the day of the play he's sucked back into his own world, but has a change of heart and returns as the curtain rises. There's a chaste kiss as the camera pulls back.

I'm light while I write it, and as I do so, I understand why I write. To write is to re-create something as you'd like it to be. I can filter my heartbreak through the giddy weightlessness of an afternoon romance movie, and suddenly it's silly. It's practically trite. My big love affair is an eighty-minute vehicle for selling tampons and life insurance.

He finds her schedules adorable. She shows him the simple pleasure of the sunrise. He shares that his cold penthouse apartment has no view at all, even being so close to the park. The first kiss is interrupted, per normal. They both change for the better.

Telling myself this story in this way confirms that it wasn't real. It was a fantasy, something I should recognize because

I'm in the fantasy business. All of that intensity and love non-sense was new to me, but to Leo it was just the drama that he brings to a part. And I'll hand it to him, he's a pro. In reality, I was living a boilerplate movie, as simple as Mad Libs. I decide I'll probably finish this one in three days, because so much of it is written for me. Easy money, I think as I lie down for my nap.

I wait until September 20 to send it to Jackie, mainly because I don't want her to know how fast I wrote it. I always think she'll negotiate for more money if she thinks it was a whole month's work. I don't wait until October 1, mainly because I don't want to put an entire mortgage payment on my credit card.

She calls me during dinner three days later. "So you fell in love with him?"

"Who?" I'm just buying time as I take my phone out to the front porch so I can have this conversation in private.

"Leo! Nora, I'm not an idiot."

"That's funny, because I am."

"Just wow. Is it all true?"

"Sort of. But in real life there was a lot of sex, and he didn't come back." I regret not bringing my wineglass outside with me.

"I'm really sorry. The agony of it comes across on the page."

"No, it doesn't." I sit up straight, defensive. "I deliberately wrote it Romance Channel style—low emotional stakes and quick resolutions."

"No, you didn't. And besides the end, which feels totally

false, this is another fantastic script. Here's my plan, I'm going to tell TRC you have the flu and push off that deadline. Then I'm going to wait until the first reviews of *The Tea House* come in, maybe October 5. If they're as good as I hope they are, I'm going to sell this for a million dollars."

"Wait. What?"

"I think *The Tea House* is going to be huge, Oscar huge. People are going to want your next script and this one is powerful. Just fix the end."

I'm so confused when I get off the phone that I go get my wineglass and the bottle and come back to the porch. It sounds like I need to reread what I sent her, maybe it wasn't as light as I'd thought. Having a film produced about how I really felt about Leo would be epically humiliating. Having a million dollars would be epically relaxing.

And then there's the trouble with the end. You can't end a movie with a woman just staring at her un-ringing phone, periodically checking on her dangling "Hey." There is no setup that allows for him to come back or for her to save face. He just left and never called again. He sent money for chrissake. No, I'd rework the bulk of the script and pull all the feeling out of it. I'd give her a dog and they'd walk the dog a lot together. Maybe she could have a secret dream to start a cupcake shop. I could take this nightmare and turn it into a TRC movie yet.

I spend a week pulling my heart out of that script. The dialogue, I hadn't noticed, was real conversations we'd had. I replace them with reflections on their hopes and dreams— he had always wanted to try woodworking. She, with the cupcake shop. Long gazes, quick brushing of hands. I make her children identical twin girls and give them all the best lines. I add a set of parents who are appropriately helpful in giving advice, but only when asked.

It takes Jackie one day to get back to me. "What the hell is this?"

"It's the TRC version of my story. Complete with a dog and cupcakes."

"So you'd rather have twenty-five thousand dollars than a million? You'd rather give up this moment where you are about to become a majorly sought-after Hollywood writer than just tell the truth?"

This wounds me a little. I like to think of myself as truthful. It felt good to write *The Tea House* because it meant something and explored the gray areas of my life. But sharing that story cost me nothing, I came out victorious in the end because I survived Ben's leaving. And I survived so well because I was so sick of him. The whole point of the story is that sometimes people leave and don't take anything with them. Leo took practically everything with him.

He took the sunrise. He took the tea house. Now he's going to take my million bucks. I think of Leo puttering around in his Bel Air mansion with Naomi, maybe planning a postshoot trip someplace tropical. I think of my credit card balance and the ugly fact that Arthur's definitely going to need braces. "Okay," I tell her. "How about this? Keep this shiny cupcake version in case we need it. Let me see if I can come up with an ending to the other one."

"Really? I'm so happy!" I can hear the cash register ring-ing in her mind. I can also see the cash advance I'm going to have to take on my eighteen percent APR credit card to make my October mortgage payment. "Let's try for mid-October. The film opens October third, so that's when the buzz will start and we'll have some idea how it's going to do. And you'll be expected at the New York opening. I forget where it is, but I'll send that to you."

"I'm not going to that."

"Nora. This is your time. You've written a really powerful script and you deserve to walk the red carpet and enjoy it. Don't let him take that from you."

I resolve not to decide. Tomorrow I'll start reworking the true script, the version called *Sunrise,* not the one called *Country Love.* I like the idea of being a serious writer and making real money. I like the idea of flying out to Hollywood to, well, I don't even know what they do out there. I'd need highlights and different clothes, and that feels good too. As long as I can keep getting men to leave me, I'll be a huge success. Shouldn't be a problem.

My kids are arguing in the living room. There's an issue with the Xbox, and I decide not to engage. "Let's all go up and brush teeth," I say.

"Fine," they say together, scowling.

When I've tucked Bernadette in, I find Arthur in bed. At the squeak of his bedroom door, he's a frenzy of sheets and something is hidden under the covers. "Oh hey, Mom," he says in a voice I don't know.

It's porn, I think. How can this be happening? He's in the sixth grade, he barely has hair on his legs. I have no man in the house to talk with him about this, and I certainly don't know where to start. For the actual first time, I kind of wish Ben was here.

I sit down on the side of his bed and give him a hug. "What's under the covers?"

"Nothing."

"It's not nothing. You had something. This is nothing to be ashamed about but we do need to talk about it. Where did you get it?"

Arthur looks at his hands. He looks at me. He starts to say something but can't.

"Sweetie, it's okay to be curious. But this isn't the way. Where'd you get it?"

"Leo," he says, and my heart stops.

Rage is beginning to spread through my chest when he pulls "it" out from under his covers and hands it to me. It's a first edition copy of *Oliver Twist*. "Oh," I say with a laugh. "Well, that's nice. Wait, when did he give you this?"

"He sent it. In the mail. At the beginning of the summer."

"Why didn't you tell me?"

Arthur waits an eternity before answering. "Because I thought it would make you sad."

"Oh, sweetie." I run my hands over his too-long hair. I touch his too-young-for-porn face. "You don't need to worry about me. I'm happy you got such a nice present."

"There was a note." He thinks before asking, "Do you want to read it?"

I think before answering, "Yes."

Dear Arthur,

Mrs. Sasaki sent me the DVD of opening night, and I've watched it twice already. You nailed it, every single line, every single song. I don't think that I could have had such command of the stage at your age. In everything you do, I hope you can own it like you did that night.

I hope you have a chance to read this book. It'll be easy, you know all the lines already. Have a fun summer and please say hi to everybody.

Love,
Leo

What the actual fuck.

THE ENDINGS TO *Sunrise* are coming at me in full force. Leo is on his way back to me but gets hit by a train. Maybe it's a slow train so it doesn't kill him right away and he's in agony living in a dirty third world hospital. He has lice. So much lice.

I want Leo to have lice and a bladder infection in the worst way. I google "can men get bladder infections?" They can! ". . . say hi to everybody." It wasn't even its own sentence. I shared half a sentence with my eight-year-old daughter, Mrs. Sasaki, Kate. Hell, everybody. We had a romance. Or at least we slept together. I should go back to *Sunrise* and read it, because I swear I'm getting confused.

No, it was a romance. At night, when he was in the tea house and I was in my room, he'd text me Miss you and all of the cells in my body would start moving at triple speed. We'd text back and forth for hours some nights, until finally I'd tell him that the sun was coming up in four hours, and that maybe we should get some sleep. He'd reply, Can't wait.

I barely slept those two weeks, except for the afternoons in the tea house. Even some of those days, I'd stay awake and watch him sleep. Isn't this how you brainwash someone? Deprive them of sleep and feed them a lot of lies? I decide I've been brainwashed and wonder how many other women have fallen for this nonsense.

When I settle on an ending to *Sunrise*, it's because it satisfies me. He's just come off a disastrous breakup with a starlet and three weeks in rehab (I've taken the liberty of ratcheting up the drinking here) and returns to my house. In my mind, his hair is infested with lice, but I don't write this because I don't want to freak out the moviegoers. He's all apologies and explanations; he finally knows what he wants.

"I know what I want too," she tells him as he holds her hand. "And it's not you."

I get up from my table in the tea house and sit on the daybed. "And it's not you," I say out loud. It feels good, this rebuke. I imagine the sting on his face. The surprise that I would have moved on, me in my little life. "And it's not you," I say again and start to cry, because of course it's not true.

CHAPTER 17

～

A WEEK BEFORE THE NEW YORK OPENING, *THE TEA House* has screened in some smaller theaters, and critics seem to like it. They call it "thoughtful" and "powerful," which is funny because I just call it "what happened." I told Jackie I'd be at the New York premiere, after she reminds me not to let Leo steal my moment in the sun.

Weezie texts me to ask if I'll be there. Who's asking? I kid.

Just me, but I want to make sure you look killer. She asks if she can have her friend, a stylist, send me a few dresses to choose from, and I figure why not. I'm not going to show up looking like I just walked off the cover of the *Tapestry* album. I have a second credit card with no balance that sort of feels like a loaded gun. I keep it in my wallet in case I need it, really need it. Ben used to count our unspent credit limit as an asset, as in, "Of course we can afford it, we have twelve hundred dollars left on the Visa."

A box arrives with three dresses and two pairs of shoes. They all have price tags on them, and I try not to look. They are emerald green, silver, and black, all fitted enough to make me look young and viable, but also tailored and lined enough to make me look like a grown-up. With Bernadette's help I choose the silver one, because she thinks it makes me look like I sparkle. The shoes are absurd and cost more than the dress. They are also silver and have the tiniest strap of leather over the toe and another around the ankle. They are nothing, weightless, yet they cost a mortgage payment. I tell Bernadette that I can just as easily wear the black shoes that I got for Granny's funeral.

"Fine." Bernadette storms out of the room and comes back with the phone. "I'm sorry, but here." She shoves the phone at me like it's medicine.

"Hello?"

"For chrissake, Nora. Just buy the shoes." *Just.*

"Hey, Pen."

"You are a big deal. You're going to the opening of your own movie. From what Bernie tells me, you're going to be gorgeous in that dress. Just for once, go the rest of the way. For me. I can't bear to think of Leo seeing you in those funeral shoes."

One thing I love about Penny is how much she cares about the stuff she cares about. The time she found white peonies for her white party. The way the new building across the street from her apartment centers perfectly in her picture window. Bernadette shares this quality, the ability to get nuclear-level excited about the smallest thing.

I try them on while we're talking. "Pen, they're the most ridiculously overpriced ounce of leather . . ." I stop talking and turn in front of the mirror.

"What?"

"They're a piece of art," I say. Is it possible that I have pretty feet? And maybe that pretty travels right up to my legs? I may be hallucinating, but I think my face might look younger. What are these, magic shoes?

"This is what I'm saying. Go big or go home. For once in your life, just buy the shoes."

"Pen, how am I going to get out of a car and walk all the way down the red carpet in these shoes?" I try to imagine it as I say it, me clunking along until that pointy heel catches a snag and I fall flat on my face, while Leo and Naomi shake their heads in pity. Penny's known me my whole life; she knows what I mean. "I have nothing to hold on to," I say.

"Well, that's bullshit, because you have me. Let me go with you to the premiere, and I'll pay for the shoes. When they see the Larson sisters all done up, Hollywood won't know what hit them."

I GET READY in my tiny bathroom with Bernadette at my elbow and Kate sitting on the side of the bathtub. There's barely enough air for the three of us, and Arthur has the good sense to wait on my bed. When my hair is blown straight and my makeup is starting to make me sweat, I shoo them all downstairs so that I can get into my dress.

I regret the dress immediately. The shimmery silver shouts,

and I realize I was hoping to move through this evening like a whisper. Or maybe I want the evening to pass without me being there at all. It's too late to right any of these decisions; I don't own another dress this fancy, and the car is coming for me in fifteen minutes.

Kate and Bernadette gasp when I come downstairs. Apparently, they love this noisy dress. Arthur is more reserved. "You look pretty, Mom. So you're just going to watch the movie and then you're coming back, right?"

Kate says, "Well, there's an after-party and who knows what else; it's New York City!" Then to me, "You go and stay out as late as you want, I've got the kids and you can grab them in the morning."

Arthur is not having this. I say, "I'm not exactly a party-all-night kind of a person; don't let this dress fool you. I'm going to watch the movie and come right back home."

"Okay, good," says Arthur. Bernadette shakes her head in disappointment.

PENNY STEPS OUT of her building in a strapless black gown and a black version of the shoes I'm wearing. She breaks into a little run when she sees me in the waiting car on the corner, and I wonder if she wears shoes like this all the time. "I am so ready," she says as she gets in the car. "Are you ready?"

"Well, I don't think I could get any more makeup on my face, so I must be ready," I say.

"You look beautiful," she says and takes my hand. "So do you know how you're going to play this? Like he's going to be there, and there's going to be a moment where you're face-to-face and you have to say something."

My hand flies up to my heart, as if to protect it, and I notice it's beating too quickly. "I'm not ready. I thought I was ready. I was going to say 'hello' and just see what he says back. That was my big plan. But no, I'm actually not ready."

"Okay, let's work backward. What do you want him to walk away thinking? That he's a jerk? That you're absolutely fine?"

I crack the window and let the fall air fill my lungs. "I want him to think I'm fine, I guess. But I don't know if I can pull it off. I'm not fine, Pen."

"Okay, we need to get your head organized. Put these things in the front: You look gorgeous in that dress. You're the reason all these people are here tonight; you wrote the thing. You're the star. He's only there because of what you created. I want to see shoulders back, forehead at rest, and a smile, like you know what I'm saying is true."

When we were little, Penny's Barbies always put their best foot forward. They were groomed and well dressed, and, no matter what kind of tragic story line I threw their way, she always had them coming out on top. Tonight, she's doing the same for me.

"Okay, I'm as gorgeous and brilliant as my shoes," I say.

"At least."

Our car has clearance to pull up right in front of the theater. Someone with a headset opens my door and helps me out. I adjust my dress and lay my black wrap over my arm. I blink into the lights. I look back and watch Penny get out of the car and notice she is smiling. I remember to do the same. We pose together for a photo and then start walking the red carpet in small steps and then normal ones. I imagine that my beautiful dress and magic shoes are a confidence costume. They are the cloak of self-assuredness, and I try to walk down the red carpet with a gait and an expression to match them. Plus, Penny is close enough to catch me if I stumble.

When we have completed our trek, I am relieved. People are milling around in the theater lobby, and someone hands us glasses of champagne off of a tray. "Nora, you look gorgeous," I hear from behind me. It's Martin. We hug hello. I introduce him to Penny, and he introduces us to his too-young wife, Candy. "This here is the next big thing in Hollywood," he tells her. "As long as she keeps writing, I'm going to be rich."

"And so is Nora," says Penny.

I thank him and down the rest of my champagne.

"Are you writing anything now?" Candy asks.

"Yes," I say and immediately wish I hadn't.

Martin claps his hands. "If this film is as well-received as I anticipate, I plan to be in a bidding war for your next project. What's it about?"

It's about Leo and me falling madly in love right after you left. It's about how the sunrise can be the most important thing in the world to a person who's lost touch with his soul. It's about a person turning his back on his soul for fame, I want to say.

"It's more nonsense about love gone wrong," I actually

say. And now I know for sure I can't let anyone read that script.

The man passes with more champagne and I take one. Of course, I haven't eaten anything since a slice of Arthur's bacon at breakfast. Stupid.

"Has Leo arrived yet?" Penny asks, and I shoot her a look that I perfected when I was twelve.

"That's probably them now," says Martin, nodding toward the mob of photographers headed toward a white limo.

As I anticipate Leo stepping out of that limo, I only know one thing: I cannot do this. What I dread most is seeing either guilt or pity on his face. It will be my undoing.

"I'm anxious to see how the movie turned out," I tell Martin. "Are we allowed to go in early and grab a good seat?"

"Sure, go ahead. We'll see you at the party after?"

"Of course," Penny answers for me. I reassure Candy that meeting her has been the highlight of my night, and we make a beeline into the theater. I lead Penny to seats in the back row in the center. I cover myself with my wrap.

"What's this?" Penny asks. "This is your big night and we're hiding back here? Take off that wrap so you can sparkle a little at least."

"I don't feel like sparkling. This was a huge mistake, Pen." I gesture toward a row of reserved seats near the front where I'm sure Leo and Naomi will be sitting.

Actual panic is creeping in. I'm not thinking about this film as much as I am about *Sunrise*. I need to take it back. I don't care so much about people knowing I had an affair with a movie star, but I do mind them knowing how much it meant to me. I can't take the chance that Leo ever sees that script, or that, God forbid, it gets made and he's cast as himself. I imagine him saying everything he ever said to me to some starlet to whom he's infinitely better suited. I imagine him reading it and thinking, *Poor thing, she had it bad.*

Heads turn toward the left theater entrance, and I know from the excitement on their faces that Leo and Naomi are walking in. I pull my wrap around me more tightly and try to make myself small. Penny takes in a breath. They make their way down to their seats and greet people as they go. He's in a tux; she's in red to match the carpet. I wonder how many haircuts he's had since I've seen him. I'm sure he's going to turn his head and see me, but instead he motions for Naomi to go first into the row of seats, leading her by the elbow and tossing her a quick smolder.

"He's about to look over here, sit up," Penny tells me out of the side of her mouth. "Act like I said something funny." I have no laugh to give, but he takes his seat without looking our way anyway.

"I have to get out of here," I say.

The look on Penny's face tells me I've probably gone white. She makes her apologies like Bugs Bunny leaving the opera as we step over people's feet to get free. She leads me out of the theater to a lobby bench. "Are you going to faint or something?" she asks. "Do you want a Coke?"

"I need to breathe, and I need to rethink everything. Literally everything." Tears start falling, and I don't even care. "I feel like I've planned a vacation to hell. Like I literally chose every flight and car ride, packed my bags, and now I'm saying, 'Wait. What am I doing in hell?'"

Penny puts her arm around me. "You kinda did."

"What was I thinking falling in love with that guy? What was I thinking writing a movie about my divorce and then showing up here tonight to watch it acted out by my old boyfriend and his girlfriend? Am I seriously supposed to watch them break up in the exact location of the last place I'll probably ever have sex?"

"You might have sex again," she says.

"And what was I thinking agreeing to do it all again? Like a whole new movie about my bad taste in men?"

"Nora?" It's Weezie with a clipboard and a sweet smile. She hands me a tissue. "You look beautiful."

"Thanks," I say. "This is my sister, Penny."

She takes a seat on the other side of me. "Too hard?"

"Too hard."

"I'm sorry. I guess I just wanted you to have that part of the movie where he sees you in your silver dress and realizes what a fool he's been."

"Me too!" says Penny. "That's all I wanted. I could taste it."

"I sort of imagined their eyes meeting as he got out of the limo," starts Weezie.

"And he'd smile softly and remember everything they had," Penny continues.

"And he'd slowly make his way over to her and touch her face. Or take her hand? I don't know exactly, but you know what I mean."

"I like that part of the movie too," I say, and they sigh. "Well, I do, and I don't. That scene is sort of an insult to both of them. Like all that's happening there is that he remembers she's pretty so he loves her again. It's not like he sees her run into a burning building to rescue an old guy. It's not like anything's changed. It's like he just got distracted by something shiny."

"Screenwriters," Weezie says and rolls her eyes.

"You can't build a life around a guy thinking you're pretty. It's not a thing."

"Okay," she says.

"It's just not enough. Don't ever settle for that."

Penny's had enough. "Weezie, we need a plan. Like, she's going to have to say hello to him at some point. I imagine the after-party's a pretty small affair. Should she call him out? Play it cool? What's your take?"

"Tell me those aren't the only two choices," I say. "I'm incapable of either of those things."

Weezie laughs. "Polite's a safe bet. You could pull that off."

Polite probably is the best way to save face. I can be polite and wish them both well and they can stop feeling sorry for me and we can all move on. But I know I can't pull it off, not even in these shoes. If I have to stand right in front of Leo and look in his eyes, I'm going to show my hand. And by "hand," I mean broken heart.

"I'm not quite there yet," I tell them. "I think I'm going to get some popcorn and we can head home."

CHAPTER 18

❧

O NE DAY I WAKE UP AND I'M A FEMINIST HERO. WHICH is funny because I'm still fantasizing about the really cute guy showing up and rescuing me from myself. *The Tea House* is being called "a primer on retaining your personal power." Women are comparing it to both their own life experiences and those of women throughout history. My favorite quote is from one of the women on *The View*: "*The Tea House* shows us that victimhood is a choice. We get to decide how we feel." What a load of crap.

People want to interview me, but I'm pretending to be reclusive and hard to get. God knows I'm not the latter. I'm afraid that if they really press me on it, I'll burst this movie's bubble. I'll have to admit that it wasn't that I refused to be a victim. It's just that I didn't care for Ben all that much.

Naomi doesn't seem to be as camera shy. She's on the daytime shows and the evening shows talking about what the film has meant to her. She looks radiant every single time. "This film was really important to me from the beginning," she tells Ellen. "I feel like if someone leaves you it's a self-correcting problem. Why would you want to be with someone who didn't want to stay?" The audience erupts with applause. Sure, take my line, because it's stupid. You'd want him to stay if you loved him. You'd want him to start loving you again so you can stop hurting. Duh, Naomi.

I have $0 in the bank and a balance of $3,463 on my credit card, and it's a week before Jackie wants to start marketing *Sunrise*. I seem to have backed myself into a bit of a corner. I need to sell this movie, but I cannot send the true story of how Leo broke my heart into the world. I also can't show the world my fantasy version, the one where Leo comes back. Nothing would make me more vulnerable than that. I'm running out of time so I start brainstorming several choppy, sentimental endings. Bernadette finds me on the porch swing with my notebook and sharp pencils after dinner. "What're you doing?"

"Trying to figure out how to end my movie."

"End it happy."

"I'm not sure this story has the ingredients for a happy ending. It's a love story, and the people aren't meant to be together."

"Can you change the ingredients?" Bernadette pulls her legs into her chest and lets me put my arm around her. She's turning nine this month and I try to imagine her as a teenager, raging against me. It doesn't seem like she has it in her.

"How do I do that?"

"Switch them up. Make them different. So that they'll end up in a different place."

"I kind of want one of them dead. Too dark?"

"Jeez, Mom. Yes. Too dark."

BERNADETTE HAS A point, though it's not until I'm in the tea house the next morning that I see it. Something needs to be switched up, and I decide to change the power structure. *She's* a pop star who comes to the country from Manhattan to film a music video on the property of a widowed father of two. They butt heads a bit but get to know each other over the duration of the shoot and fall in love. She even offers to help with his daughter's school chorus concert.

I leave in all the feelings. She tells him, in a clearing full of birds, that he's the first man she's ever been in love with. He believes her and thinks it's forever. In the end, he's the one who's abandoned. I'm going to ghost him.

And then it can have a happy ending. She'll write a song for him, and he'll hear it on the radio driving down a country road, and he'll know that she really loves him. She'll win a Grammy for it and mention him in her acceptance speech. Then the next day he comes home from whatever he does all day and finds her strumming her guitar on his front porch. Big moment, big kiss. It seems to work when I'm in charge.

IT'S NOVEMBER AND I've sold *Sunrise* to Purview Pictures for $750,000. Martin has signed on as director, and they're starting casting soon. I ask Jackie if I can cash my check and not have anything more to do with the film. I have the right to be on set, which they tell me will be in Mississippi, but I have no intention of going.

I have money now, and I like it. I can't get over the fact that I actually made that much money, like I made it out of nothing but words and heartbreak. I want having that money to be worth it, so after paying my credit card bill I let the rest of it sit in my account for a while and try to decide what to do with it.

On a Thursday night, after *Wheel of Fortune,* I scroll through Leo's Instagram feed one last time. Movie promotion, fancy-looking cheeseburger, a sideline shot of a football player I don't recognize. When I'm done, I ceremonially delete the Instagram app and move my banking app to the exact spot where it used to sit. I get in bed and scroll through my account. The big deposit, the interest. It's infinitely satisfying, and I wish there was a LIKE button to press.

My parents aren't necessarily frugal people. And Penny certainly isn't. I came by my spartan ways out of necessity. Every time I would get ahead financially, Ben would go on some kind of bender. I never knew when it was going to happen, so I learned to live in a state of preparedness. Buy the chicken on sale because Ben might decide he needs flying lessons. Let the hem out of Bernadette's Easter dress because Ben might decide he wants office space. I am not covering for Ben anymore, I remind myself. It's my own money. When I wake up in the morning, it's right there where I left it.

I call Penny to discuss this, because she's the only person

I know with this kind of money. "Money's energy," she tells me. I roll my eyes because I know this is going to be like the time she told me to move my bed to another wall to improve my sex life. I should probably tell her that the real fix was moving Ben to another continent. "You sent your heartbreak out into the world, and it brought you money. Now before you send the money back out, try to imagine the feelings you want it to bring." Oh brother.

"Pen. Seriously." This is the last brand of crap I want to listen to right now.

"I'm dead serious. And you need to be honest. What you want is to feel the way you felt when Leo was there."

"You want me to pay Leo to come back?" Honestly, sometimes she makes me a little violent.

"No, just replicate the feelings. Think about it, even just for a day. How do you want to feel?" We hang up after I tell her I love her even though she has no concept of reality, and she replies that we create our own reality. We end many, many conversations this way.

But I give it some thought. It might be worth thinking about how I want to feel, because I've really burned out on feeling the way I currently feel. My first thought is that I want to feel secure, like the future is solid, so I open college accounts for my kids. This is something I never thought I'd be able to do, and I luxuriate in it. I replace the sleepless nights that I spent worrying about the future with daydreams about how that future might be. It's possible that I'm two inches taller standing on solid ground.

There's another feeling though, a little harder to face. At

Penny's suggestion, I think about how it felt when Leo was here. Not the feeling of being loved—I hear you can't buy that—but just the feeling that it's okay to enjoy nice things. I liked the better wine and the nicer sheets. I really like those new towels. I liked letting go of my prairie woman mentality and enjoying something as frivolous as lights hanging over a picnic table. With Ben, nice things meant we were about to go without. They felt like an assault on my hard work, a punishment. With Leo, nice things weren't so loaded. They were just nice.

So I hire a contractor to start renovations on my house. He's not to touch the porch or the tea house, but we design a new kitchen where everything works and add a powder room on the first floor. I order new windows that look exactly like the original ones but are airtight. Suddenly my house is stronger and so am I for having taken care of it. Money, I decide, is not evil.

ON NOVEMBER 22 at two A.M., I get a text. The chime wakes me up and I'm sure someone's dead. It's Leo: How could you write this?

My heart races. The last text I have from him is when we were still in the bubble. I love you. I miss you. Love you too. Followed by my eternally dangling Hey. And now right under it, all these months later, he's back.

Me: Sunrise?

Leo: Yes, fucking Sunrise. You took the whole thing and packaged it and sold it. How did you think I was going to feel when I read it?

196

Me: Why are you reading it?

Leo: They sent it to me to see if I want the part. To play you, I guess

Me: Ha. Walk a mile in my shoes

Leo: You're ruthless

Me: I literally don't know what you're talking about

Leo: It mattered and you turned it into one of your bullshit stories. I'm surprised you didn't give yourself a cupcake shop

Me: Leo you're the one who left

Leo: I was coming back

A thousand replies run through my mind: Have you been
in traffic for seven months? Were you incarcerated? Side-
tracked? Sleepy? Goofy? Before I've chosen one, he texts:

Leo: Forget it. I'm glad you're happy. Go back to sleep.

I wait for another text. I have the feeling of just having
woken up from a dream where I'm trying to sort disjoined
fragments into a narrative.

I type: Why didn't you come back? But erase it. I type: I am
happy, and hit SEND. I say this in part because I don't want
him feeling sorry for me and also because it's nearly true, I'm
not too far from happy. I've gotten through the worst of this
heartbreak. I'm getting a new kitchen. Arthur has friends in
middle school and a part in the winter play.

I sense that he's gone. I type: Leo? And it turns out I'm
right.

The nice thing about a text exchange is that there's an of-
ficial transcript. I read the whole thing over and over again.
In the morning I screenshot it and send it to Kate.

"Was there any indication while you were together that
maybe he's psychotic?"

197

"Seriously. I thought the same thing. 'I was coming back.' I mean you don't call, you don't text, and then in the end you don't come back, so what does 'I was coming back' mean? I've seen him on TV and in person, actually; he hasn't lost both of his legs."

"I wondered about that too," Kate says. *"An Affair to Remember.* But I didn't want to say anything. Maybe he's a narcissist."

"Maybe," I say. "Do you even know what that means?"

"I do not," she consents.

"Me either." We laugh.

"It could be that the technical term is 'asshole,'" she says.

"Maybe."

"He tells you you're the first woman he's ever been in love with while he's nursing a broken heart over Naomi. Then leaves you to go back to her and accuses you of being heartless. There's a diagnosis in there somewhere."

"Did I tell you my contractor's kind of cute?" I say.

"Oh, here we go."

CHAPTER 19

❧

MY KITCHEN IS DONE BY CHRISTMAS AND EVERYTHING looks beautiful. I have freshly painted cabinets, new appliances, and a shiny marble countertop. When I press the button to run my dishwasher, it runs. Every single time. When I turn the knob on one of my burners, there's fire. No matches. I walk down my still rickety stairs each morning and gasp at my good fortune. My kids still sit in the exact same spot and eat the exact same food, but they appreciate the fact that the December chill stays outside. Even though they're sick of people talking about me and my movie, I can tell they're proud of me. My contractor was, in fact, cute and also single, but he had a way of over pronouncing his G's when using the gerund tense that I just couldn't get past. It's possible I'm not ready to move on.

My parents come for four days and stay in Arthur's room, because he has the double bed. I delight in having him bunk in with me. He's on the verge of shutting down the cuddling, as I am sure is appropriate, and I wonder if each time is the last. We're reading *Harry Potter*, which I find shockingly lacking in romance.

My dad calls me "Hollywood" now. As in, "Hey, Hollywood, want to scramble me up some eggs?" They're excited for me but also worried. They run their hands over my new countertops and ask if I've saved any for a rainy day. I assure them that I have.

"So what's next?" my mom asks over Christmas Eve dinner.

"Dessert," Bernadette tells her.

My mom laughs. "No, I mean big picture. Are you writing something new? Are you strictly writing for the big screen now?"

"I'm not sure. I'm thinking of writing something that's not romance for a change. Like friendship or murder."

Arthur's looking down at his plate. I say, "Or adventure. Arthur, you could help me with that." He looks up but doesn't speak. "Sweetie? You okay?"

"What do you think Dad and Leo do on Christmas?" Dad and Leo. In his mind, it's one thing.

If I speak, I'll cry. My mom knows this and fills the room with words. This is one of the best parts of my mom, her ability to fill a space with words that will take things in a new direction. I remember getting a tooth pulled as a child and my mother sitting in the chair behind the dentist, telling the story of a rooster she met on her way to church last week.

"Well," she starts, "your dad is in Asia, I assume, cele-

NORA GOES OFF SCRIPT

brating Christmas in an old Buddhist temple. He's eating rice and trying to convince his friends that eggnog isn't disgusting. Which it is." She gives Arthur a sideways smile and my heart starts to loosen up.

"Do Leo," says Bernadette. "Where's he?"

"Oh poor Leo, he's celebrating Christmas in Mexico. Cabo San Lucas to be exact. He's joined up with a traveling mariachi band who make him carry all their luggage because he doesn't know how to play the guitar. I'm afraid he's getting a sunburn."

Arthur laughs, to my great relief, and we go through all of our other friends and family who aren't with us. Penny's coming from the city with her family tomorrow for Christmas lunch, so my mom tells us that tonight she and Rick are at McDonald's loading up on Big Macs.

Penny at McDonald's sends us all into peals of laughter. In fact, in that moment as I'm opening a second bottle of wine, I think that Penny at McDonald's has saved our Christmas. I smile my appreciation at my mom and pour us each another glass.

Santa's bringing Arthur the new bike he's been asking for for two years. It was available in a box or fully assembled for an extra fifty bucks. I splurged. He's bringing Bernadette this horrible doll world that she'd asked for that comes in a thousand tiny pieces for her to put together. I find myself in the sunroom with my parents and the Christmas tree, with absolutely nothing to assemble after my kids have gone to bed.

My dad asks, "So no word from either of them?"

"I must be really scary," I say.

"I didn't know this Leo of course, but Ben was a jerk."

I raise my glass. "Hear, hear."

We sit and look at the tree. My mom has texted Penny twice to remind her to bring snow pants and boots for the boys so that they can play outside after lunch. She thinks we don't notice, but it is her mission to loosen them up every time she sees them, to wrinkle their starched shirts at a minimum. My mom believes that it's a kid's job to get as dirty as possible for bath time every day. I am overwhelmed by how much I love my parents.

I may be tipsy because instead of responding to that, I pull out my phone. "Can I show you guys something?"

I squeeze between them on the couch so we can all look at my phone. "Leo texted me last month." I pull up the conversation and wish they didn't have to see the I love you. I miss you from May. Not to mention my love you too and the dangling Hey.

My mom catches her breath. "You loved him? He loved you?"

"I guess," I say and proceed to read them the conversation. I explain that *Sunrise* is loosely based on our relationship. They ask me to read the conversation again.

I return to my chair because I'm feeling too constrained between the two of them. They're looking too closely at my life and I'm sure they can read my mind. My dad has his hands folded on his belly, and he's staring out the window at the tea house. "You're missing something."

"Yes," my mom agrees.

"The ability to hang on to a man?" I ask.

NORA GOES OFF SCRIPT

"I don't know what it is, and I wouldn't make yourself crazy trying to figure it out," he says. Which, too late. "But there's a missing link out there. I wish he had the balls to tell you what it is."

We are quiet. My mom asks, "He's not going to star in the movie, is he?"

"No, he turned it down. They cast Peter Harper."

My mom claps her hands. "Peter Harper! Darling, you must have an affair with him too!"

"Marilyn, honestly," my dad says.

CHAPTER 20

I T'S JANUARY AND MY PHONE RINGS WHILE I'M WATCHING the sunrise. I'm wearing a coat and a wool hat and two sweaters over my pajamas. The January sunrise is lower than the others, a quieter drama but a drama nonetheless.

"Holy shit," says Jackie. "Are you sitting down?"

"Why do people ask that?"

"*The Tea House* has been nominated for four Academy Awards, including Best Original Screenplay."

I'm silent.

"That's you. You've been nominated for an Academy Award."

"What about Leo?"

"He's nominated for Best Actor. Naomi was snubbed. Martin is nominated, as well as Best Original Score, which, to be honest I don't even remember."

"Wow."

"Yeah, this is really huge for us, Nora. Huge. You'd better start writing."

"Can I call you back?" I ask, already hanging up. The sun's coming up and I want to focus on it. Same sunrise, slightly different because I've been nominated for an Oscar.

My hands are texting Leo. Congratulations.

You too, I get back immediately. Sun up yet?

Halfway.

Send me a photo? So I do.

What the hell is that?

It's called January. They don't have that in L.A.?

I'm in New York. I freeze at the closeness of him. I'd been picturing him in L.A., if I have to admit that I am occasionally picturing him. It hadn't occurred to me that he was ninety minutes away. *Come over?* I want to type, but don't.

I think the conversation is over, as I can't come up with a retort for his being in New York, but then there are bubbles. So what have you been up to?

Talk about a broad question. Being a mom? Shoveling snow? Making meatloaf? Trying not to think about you? Selling pain for cash, mostly, I say finally.

Ha. I think you owe me a cut.

I redid my kitchen.

Oh.

It was rude that you sent me all that money, I hope you know I sent it back. I don't know where this is coming from, but apparently I need to get that off my chest.

I was just trying to make it seem like I was a renter

You were my lover

No kidding. I thought I was covering for you

I've got to go. Excited to tell the kids.

Ok I guess I'll see you guys there.

Where

At the Oscars, Nora.

I need to wake up my kids. It's a Monday and I've sat on the porch way too long. First, texting Leo, then my parents, Penny, and Kate. Kate's going to take me to lunch to celebrate and also run through this last text conversation for logic.

Bernadette screams when I tell her. Like a real live high-pitched little girl scream. Arthur throws his body around me.

"Mom, I knew this was going to happen. I knew you could do it."

"I see you in lavender," Bernadette tells me. "But with a spray tan and some highlights."

"Are you trying to turn me into Writes-A-Lot Barbie?"

Celebratory pancakes are followed by celebratory drop-off and a celebratory run. I meet Kate at the café. She's waiting with two glasses of champagne. "I can't freaking believe it."

"Same." We toast to that and laugh.

"So what did he say?"

I hand her my phone.

"What was he 'covering for you' for?"

"No idea." I pick at my Cobb salad. "Like, is he protecting me from people finding out we were shacked up? I wrote a movie about it for chrissake. What do I care?"

"I'd tell everybody," says Kate.

"I can't decide whether to focus on this, the most exciting moment of my career, maybe life. Or the fact that I'm going to see him."

"I'd be focused on seeing him," she says as she spears a piece of shrimp. "Though you need to psych yourself up so you don't freak out like last time."

"This feels different. Like last time I saw the two of them I was terrified they'd turn and see me and feel sorry for me. Now that it seems like he's borderline angry at me, I feel kinda like a badass."

"Maybe you actually dumped him, but you blacked out."

"That doesn't happen, though I like the thought," I say.

When I get back in the car I have a series of all-caps texts from Weezie. To summarize, she's really happy for me, and if I haven't started looking for a dress yet, I'm already behind schedule.

I agonize over who to bring with me. The simplest answer is to go alone, but what if I win and I have strangers on either side. Who do I hug? Of course I'm not going to win, but one has to be prepared. I have a lifelong recurring dream that I am about to give a speech that I've known about for a long time, and I've forgotten to prepare anything. In the Oscar situation, I'm told I'll have thirty seconds, which is twenty-five too many anyway. I resolve to memorize three sentences so that I won't have to resort to notes. I always wonder at actors who thank the six people in the world they are most grateful for and have to look at an index card to remember their names.

I call Jackie and share my concern about who to bring, and she calls Martin. Apparently, this is her first brush with the Oscars too. It turns out Martin and Candy are separated and I could go as his date. He thinks it's cleaner for the movie if we don't dilute our block of seats with dates. "Leo and Naomi will be going together," she tells me.

Naturally.

My parents want to come, which sort of feels like it's complicating things, but it's fun that they're so excited. Martin says he can get them tickets and an invitation to the *Vanity Fair* party. Penny makes us an appointment at Bergdorf Goodman to try on dresses. My dad springs for a new tux.

Everything suddenly feels like I'm getting married, and I resist the urge to cycle between remembering my actual wedding to Ben and imagining I'm flying out to marry Leo.

The dress lady's name is Olympia, and she escorts my mom, Penny, and me into a large dressing room and offers us champagne. Bernadette is at school, probably still livid that she's missing this. Olympia brings in four black dresses for my mom before she accepts the fact that my mom lives in Technicolor.

"I'm almost seventy years old," my mom tells her, "and I've never even been to California. This is the biggest moment of my life. I want to be in yellow, like a lemon on a tree."

Penny and I smile at each other, because my mom is adorable. I don't know what Pantone's saying about the color of the year, but there's no chance there's a wide selection of yellow dresses for women of a certain age.

Olympia is thrilled. "Oh yay! I was worried you were a bore. I'll be right back. And, Nora, what about you?"

"My daughter wants me in lavender," I say. "But I'm open to suggestions." Olympia claps her hands.

When she's gone, Penny says, "I'm overthinking the dress. I know I am. I just want Leo to look at you and drop dead from regret. Like I want him to stand and weep. Is that too much to ask?"

"Probably," I say.

"Like I imagine you in a skintight gold dress that leaves nothing to the imagination. And his jaw dropping to the ground. All of it caught on camera."

My mom is laughing. "Penny, I don't know how it ever happened that you're not the romance writer."

"I've given this some thought too," I say, which is the biggest understatement of all time. "And the last thing I want is to put myself in a beauty competition with Naomi. And I don't believe that Leo would fall back in love with me just because I look good. He's not that kind of person, and I wouldn't want him if he was. Painful truth, right there. I just want to show up looking like myself and feeling comfortable so I can enjoy the whole thing."

Penny sighs. "Fine. You can look like yourself, but we'll fix you up a little."

My mom ends up with a canary-yellow chiffon gown with long billowing sleeves. She looks like old Hollywood, glamorous in a carefree kind of way. I am more excited seeing my mom in this dress than I have been since I got the call.

In a stroke of good luck, they have one lavender dress, and I happen to love it. It has a wide scoop neck that shows off my collarbones (take that, Leo) and hangs in heavy crepe to the floor. It fits where it should, but nothing pulls, nothing grabs. It's completely comfortable. When I put it on, my mom says, "That's the one. I like the way you feel in it."

Over meatloaf, the week before the event, Bernadette has a million questions. I've already answered most of them. Will there be snacks? What if I get cold? Who will drive me to the party after? Have I practiced walking up stairs in my shoes?

Arthur is quiet. "Are you worried about this, Arthur? I don't expect to win, I just think it'll be fun to get dressed up and be on TV."

"Will Leo have a date?" he asks.

"He'll be with Naomi Sanchez, his co-star." And I'm not

sure why I say it this way, as if Arthur is going to be upset that she's his girlfriend.

"I bet he liked hanging out with you more than he likes hanging out with her."

Bernadette and I both look at him, surprised. This isn't something we really talk about anymore, but it sort of feels like he's been stewing about it for a while. "Well, who wouldn't?" I say, and I'm rewarded with a smile.

"Poor Naomi," Bernadette kids.

"She's a real charity case," I say.

CHAPTER 21

I'S THE END OF FEBRUARY AND I WAKE UP IN THE BEVERLY Hills Hotel. Because I'm an Oscar nominee, I remind myself. I go to my balcony to see if I can see the sunrise, but I can't. Los Angeles seems to center entirely around the sunset. I make myself a cup of coffee and look over the treetops.

I am happy, I think. Whenever I remember to think of the things I'm grateful for, my health, my kids, and the sunrise have been top of the list. Throw in my house, and I really have nothing to complain about. Even when Ben was around and belittling me for selling out and writing crappy romance movies, I felt grateful for my work. I mean someone had to sell out, you can't walk into the Stop n' Save and trade big ideas for chicken.

But this. To have written a screenplay that is essentially my truth, or at least represents my feelings about my truth, and to have it produced and then appreciated. It's almost too much for me to contain at this moment. What if people like *Sunrise*? What if this is my new normal—showing people my heart and having them applaud it?

And as for my heart, it's okay. I've read that quote a million times, the one about knowing when to let go of things that were not meant for you. Leo was not meant for me. I mean, look at him. We had a moment, and it was perfect. Can't I just leave it at that? Encapsulate the memory and protect it? Maybe the whole thing was just a dream, anyway. Frankly, if his sheets weren't sitting on Kate's guest room bed, I might actually think I made the whole thing up.

I go for a run through the flats of Beverly Hills and meet my parents at In-N-Out Burger for lunch. I want real food in my stomach tonight; I want to feel solid. "I hope your fairy godmother's bringing backup," my dad jokes as I wipe the grease off my face with the last napkin. I'm in my most comfortable jeans and an over-washed sweatshirt.

"Charlie!" my mom admonishes with a grin.

"You think I'm going to have a chance to meet Leo?" my dad asks.

"Maybe. But if you do, just pretend he's any guy, like this never happened. No questions. No innuendos."

"Oh, I've got questions all right. Putz."

This feels like a real wild card. "Dad, let's all just act like he's a guy who showed up to celebrate my big night. We're not mad at him. We're not intimidated by him. We're just happy, neutral people who have moved on."

"I'm not an actor, sweetheart."

THE GLAM SQUAD shows up at my room and they blow out my hair and curl the ends, making me look like I didn't have my hair done but that I'm just a person with good hair. This is what I asked them for.

Someone shows up with a spray tan tent. "Weezie sent me," she says. I tip her and send her home. This is the color I am, I'm afraid. I tell the makeup lady that I don't feel comfortable in makeup, that she needs to go on the light side.

"They all say that," she says.

"But I mean it."

She rolls her eyes. "You need to look like a cheap stripper in real life so that you don't look like a corpse on camera. Can you just trust me?"

No, not at all. "Sure," I say.

My dress is hanging on the back of the bathroom door. I love this dress. I asked for lavender to please Bernadette and also to not seem too overt. This dress is simple enough that it doesn't shout anything, but it makes me feel like I'm beautiful in my own right. My shoes are the same exquisite silver ones I wore to the film premiere when I made my Cinderella exit.

When I am ready, I feel ready. Martin is picking me up, and all I need to do is get my body into the lobby. This is not my world, and I could easily shrink from the magnitude of this thing, but I keep repeating to myself, "I'm nominated." It's not just like I was invited to this party; the party's for me.

Martin gets out of the limo to help me in. "Well, look who got out of the sticks."

"Me," I say and kiss him on the cheek. When we're settled and I've re-smoothed my dress several times, I say, "How do you think we'll do tonight?"

"I have absolutely no way of knowing. *Wartime Sisters* could knock us out. Or it couldn't. Any one of us winning is a win though; we'll always be referred to as Academy Award–winning *The Tea House*. Even if it's just that dull musical score."

I look out the window.

"Were you in love with him?"

"Yes," I say after a while. I smile. "I'm fine now."

We're silent for a while before I ask, "Does Naomi know?"

"I don't think so. Eventually she'll see *Sunrise*, and she'll know." How have I never thought of this? Is this going to cause a problem between Leo and her? I decide that I don't really care, that he deserves it. And at least she wasn't cast for the part. I'm grateful that I don't have to watch the great love story of my life play out with the great love of his life in the leading role.

We're here. Martin knows that this is more nerve-racking to me than it is to him. He takes my hand. "I'm going to get out first and then help you out. People are going to be taking pictures so your best look is shoulders back and a mild Mona Lisa smile. A real smile and you end up looking like the Joker in the papers." Unfortunately, this makes me smile for real. I try to contain myself.

Walking the red carpet is exactly what you'd expect. I'm sure I've watched the past thirty-five Academy Awards ceremonies on TV, and there are no surprises. Fans seem to know who Martin is, and I assume they think I'm his date. There's a logjam where some of us are supposed to wait to talk with whoever's replaced Joan Rivers. I can't remember who I'm wearing, and I hope they won't ask.

There's a hand on my elbow, and I know it's him. I turn around and face him, glad I've opted for the too-high version of these shoes and that my collarbones are exposed.

"Hi," I manage.

"You look beautiful," he says.

"Thanks. It's a lot of smoke and mirrors." I indicate the dress, the hair, the tiny handbag. Anything to break the tension of this moment because any more eye contact and I'm going to start to cry.

Martin is now at my side, protective. "Best-looking date I've ever brought to one of these things—am I right, Leo?"

"Careful," he says. "She'll break your heart."

And suddenly I understand rage. I understand setting fires and smashing in people's faces with iron knuckles. I ball up my fists and search my rage for the right words when Naomi approaches and breaks my focus. She is ethereal in a white silk gown. I'm preoccupied with whether or not she's wearing underwear. I'm one hundred percent sure she didn't have a burger for lunch.

"Nora!" She kisses the air by my face, not because she's an insincere person, I actually don't think she is, but because the makeup situation is so intense.

"You look absolutely stunning," I tell her. I'm back on the high road, and honestly what else could I say? She glows.

"Well, good luck tonight," she says to Martin and me, holding Leo's arm. "Good luck to all of us, I guess."

The assistant from the E! channel approaches to bring Leo and Naomi for a quick interview. Leo gives her his full attention and a quick smolder. She goes red and starts to talk at triple speed. "Okay, okay, so just this way, you two were so great in that movie, okay, okay . . ." Leo turns and has the absolute freakin' nerve to give me a wink.

MY AWARD IS early, because no one really cares about the screenplay category. I'm glad we'll get it over with so that I won't have to be nervous for the rest of the show. I'm not nervous about winning and having to get up there onstage, I've managed my expectations. I'm nervous about the part where they show the faces of the nominees on TV as they announce them and then show them again when they name the winner. I've been unable to decide how my face is supposed to go. Mona Lisa smile? Glee? When they announce Barry Sterns's name as the winner (that's who I'd pick), do I nod in agreement and applaud? I decide that's what Meryl Streep would do. Nod and applaud. That's the gracious way out.

Martin and I are on the aisle in the second row. Leo and Naomi are directly in front of us in today's episode of fresh hell. They look so right together, like they should be the models for all of the wedding-cake toppers in all the world. They must be in that comfortable silence part of the relationship, because they don't speak.

Peter Harper from *Sunrise* is announcing the category. His press people have been trying to get him everywhere in anticipation of that film coming out later this year. His last film, *Shrapnel*, a World War II piece, got him a lot of attention and a quick relationship with a swimsuit model.

He comes out in a tuxedo and says some words about the importance of story. I'm underwater now and can't really hear anything. "The nominees are," he starts, and Martin pinches me, actually pinches me. I turn to him and see his best Mona Lisa smile, which I gratefully replicate. I breathe.

"And the Oscar goes to . . . Nora Hamilton, for *The Tea House*." I hear this and Mona Lisa is gone. I beam with what must be Bernadette's smile, and I can only imagine my kids at Penny's house jumping up and down on the couch.

I am being hugged by Martin. He whispers in my ear, "You have to go up now," so I do. This part is not what I imagined from watching it on TV. The steps are treacherous, though I manage them by lifting the front of my dress and walking too slowly. Peter Harper is at least three inches shorter than I imagined, and he kisses my cheek as he hands me the statue. It's heavy, just like they say.

I am at the podium and there are so many more people there than I could have imagined. Thirty seconds count down on the clock, and my three sentences are lost to me. Leo is in the front row and gives me a smile, his real smile, and the surprise of it brings me to.

I ad-lib. "I am really grateful that I had the opportunity to tell this story. And I'm more grateful that it was welcomed, nurtured, and performed by such talented people. It's wonderful to speak your truth and be heard. Thank you all."

And now Peter Harper has his arm around my waist and he's leading me offstage. I didn't thank Martin or shout out to my kids or even mention the Academy. I now see what the deal is with the index cards.

I return to my seat at the commercial break, and Naomi hugs me and says all the right things. Leo says, "I knew it," and gives me his real smile again.

"Don't do that," I say, too quickly.

The orchestra starts and someone's coming out to introduce a dance number. I can feel my phone blowing up in my tiny bag. I can feel the weight of this gorgeous statue on my lap. I see Leo whisper something to Naomi that makes her smile. Life really is a mixed bag.

Martin wins and thanks me for such a heartfelt story. Leo wins and says, "And I'd like to thank Nora Hamilton for the story and for letting us overstay our welcome in her tea house." This makes me cry, and I know that he sees. I fish in my bag for a tissue, more to protect my makeup than my pride. *You were welcome to stay,* I want to say. *I might have even let you start sleeping inside.*

When it's over we pose for photos. They want Martin, Leo, and me all with our Oscars against the logo backdrop. "Can you move in a bit closer, Mr. Vance?" asks the photographer. "Maybe put your arm around her?" He puts his arm around my waist instead of my shoulders and pulls me close to him. This takes me by surprise, and I turn to look up at him. The camera flashes, and I think this is the photo that will make it into all the press. The one with me looking up at Leo like he's the prom king.

CHAPTER 22

❦

AT THE *VANITY FAIR* PARTY, I SORT OF FLOAT AROUND. The Oscar I'm carrying shouts, "Talk to me! It's important that you know me!" I meet directors and producers and actors that I've been watching for decades. I drink champagne and eat off of passed trays while people take turns carrying my Oscar. It's just been engraved with my name so I assume it'll make its way back to me. I keep an eye out just in case.

I don't see Leo, and I try not to look for him. Or, rather, I tell myself I'm looking for my parents while actually looking for him. I wander around with Martin, meeting everyone he wants me to meet. I feel comfortable in a way I couldn't have imagined; winning has emboldened me. There is nothing I can do to wipe the smile off of my face as people congratulate me and I sip champagne. "Hello. Thank you. Nice to meet you." I love this night.

Martin wants me to meet someone named Cayla who doesn't seem old enough to babysit. "This right here," he tells me, "is my next big star." Cayla giggles, and I drain my glass so I have a reason to walk away.

I'm waiting at the bar when my mind starts playing tricks on me. How many glasses of champagne have I had, I wonder. Leo is standing next to me. "You must be Nora," he says, which makes no sense. This Leo is slightly taller with shorter hair. "I'm Luke Vance. The brother."

"I really thought I was drunk there for a second," I say, because my filter is not working. "I mean you really look a lot alike. Wow." I shake his hand.

"Congratulations," he says. "You guys really swept it tonight. We cheered you on from the nosebleed seats."

"Thanks. I still can't believe it." There's more of an ordinariness to Luke, which I find refreshing. Like Luke's been to Costco. He's as handsome as Leo, but he doesn't seem to expect anyone to notice. He has Leo's way of looking at you as if you have all of his attention, which I find slightly painful. I wonder if this is something they picked up from their parents. "I'm sorry about your mom," I say.

He's taken aback, and I resolve not to finish this glass. "Thank you. Leo never talks about it. I guess I shouldn't be surprised that he told you."

A pretty, dark-haired woman rushes over to us and puts her arm through Luke's. "Oh, I don't want to miss this. I'm Jenn. I've been dying to meet you." She's out of place in her normalness, like we're at a barbecue. I like her immediately.

She congratulates me, which isn't getting old. She says she

likes my dress, which isn't getting old. And then, "You really got to him. Luke and I never thought it would happen. All these starlets rolling through year after year, and it's a real woman—a mom even—who does him in." Luke's nodding as she says this, like this is the thing they were just talking about on the drive over. And also like this is a fun fact, rather than the saddest thing in the world.

An older man hands Jenn a margarita before turning his smile on me. "Ah, here she is. I'm William Vance, their father. I thought it was a great film, congratulations." There's a hairline crack in my heart as I look at Leo's dad. It's like looking at future Leo, the one I'm not going to grow old with. Seeing his dad also rounds him out, like he's a guy with a past and parents. I briefly want him to be held accountable.

"You're all so handsome," I hear myself saying as we shake hands.

William laughs. "Well, thank you. Luke and I are just handsome as a hobby. Only Leo makes a living at it." Luke and Jenn laugh, so I do too. These are some of the easiest people I've ever met. They're grounded and open, like the best parts of Leo. And they don't think Leo can handle hospice.

Leo appears and gives them each a hug. "Thanks for coming. I see you met Nora."

"She lives up to your description," Luke says, and Leo winces. He's visibly uncomfortable. I wonder if he seriously thinks I'm going to call him out for dumping me, right here in front of everyone. I think we've established that I'm not exactly the kind of person who calls people out.

People seem to be inching closer to us as I stand and stare

at these two brothers, one who is Leo and one who is not. I must look confused, because Luke laughs and says, "He got drunk at Thanksgiving and told us the whole story."

"You did?" I'm looking straight at Leo, but he won't look at me.

"Maybe," says Leo. "Hard to remember."

"At Thanksgiving," I say. What I really want to say is *What's "the whole story"? Can you explain it to me?*

"Leo brought a bottle of scotch and finished it. Performance of his life," William says.

"Wish I could have seen it," I say, mostly to myself.

"It sounds beautiful, where you live," Jenn says to me.

"Okay, wow, fun that you guys are here," Leo says, "but we don't need to do this. It's fine. What happens at Thanksgiving stays at Thanksgiving, right?"

"I taught Leo how to grocery shop," I say. "I was like a counselor at Camp Normal Life, and he did pretty well." I've had exactly the right amount of champagne to want to keep this going, as it turns out.

Now he's looking right at me, hard. "Please," he says.

A flourish of yellow appears out of the corner of my eye. My parents are standing a few feet away, unsure if it's okay to approach. The only thing in the world that could make this situation more awkward is Leo meeting my parents. This certainly isn't how I dreamed of it happening. My dad makes eye contact and approaches, dragging my mom with him.

"Leo," he says, extending his hand more formally than I'd expect. "Charlie Larson. Nora's father." There's something in the way he enunciates the word "father" that makes it sound like a threat.

Leo is completely flustered, and this makes Luke smile. "Oh, sir, nice to meet you. And are you Marilyn?" He shakes their hands, holding my mom's between his for a beat longer than necessary. "So nice to meet you. I'm a big fan of your grandkids."

"So we've heard," says my dad. I need to make this stop.

I introduce them to Luke, Jenn, and William. And I eye my mom, willing her to fill the space. She delivers. "Well, this has been the single most exciting night of my entire life. My daughter wins an Oscar and accepts it so beautifully. You really did look beautiful up there, sweetheart. And then just now I walked out of the bathroom and right into Dirk Richardson! He was just standing right there, like he was waiting for me. I don't know what came over me but I said, 'Dirk, I'm Marilyn' because I've seen every one of his movies and I feel like I've known him my whole life. And he took my hand and said, 'Hello, Marilyn.' Can you imagine that?"

"And now I've got to go find him and punch his lights out," my dad kids. They're smiling at each other and I can feel Leo looking my way. I don't dare look at him in case he can still read my mind. My parents are the happy ending of the romance movie. My parents are what we could have been if he'd just come back.

"Martin wanted to meet you guys," I tell them. "Let's go find him before he runs off with a teenager." Everyone exchanges good-byes and nice-to-meet-yous. William hugs me, like hard. As I usher my parents off to find Martin, or anyone for that matter, I realize that Leo and I are the only two who didn't say good-bye. I guess that's just our thing.

IT'S NEARLY MIDNIGHT, and I'm in the bathroom happily noticing that most of my makeup has worn off. I'm sick of all this hair on my shoulders and wish I had a pencil to secure it in a knot. I check my phone and see that everyone I've ever met has texted me, including Ben: I must be a hell of a muse, I've got to see this movie! That's as close to "congratulations" as Ben's going to get.

"There you are," says Naomi, coming out of a stall. "You must feel like a million bucks."

"It does feel pretty good, I have to say. I never saw it coming."

"Well, it was a powerful story, I think you helped a lot of women by telling it." She's reapplying her lipstick, which seems like a normal thing to do, so I pull out mine.

"Thanks." That's all I should say, but I'm a little cracked open after seeing so much of Leo tonight. I'm raw all over again, and I just want to hear all the facts so I can reseal my heart. "So what do you and Leo do now? Stay in L.A.?"

"I think Leo's headed back to New York, but I'm not sure. I'm going to France. I'm going to take a full month off to read and eat delicious things."

My envy is profound, but this whole scenario sounds like it would be better with Leo. "He didn't want to come?"

"Who?"

"Leo."

She laughs. "Leo and I wouldn't even share a coffee together, let alone a month's getaway. Neither of us would survive." She's dusting her face with powder and stops. "Nora. You don't think Leo and I are a thing? Tell me you don't."

"Aren't you?"

"That's movie promotion. If people are gossiping about us, the movie gets mentioned. That's pretty much Hollywood 101."

"Oh." I feel like someone who just wandered off the Kansas cornfields onto Hollywood Boulevard. "But you were together before, right?"

"Like for a minute. But it was nothing. Look, Leo's super attractive, but we literally have nothing to talk about. It got old fast."

We had everything to talk about, I want to say. How is that possible? He's got nothing to say to her but can talk to me for twenty hours a day and pick up in the morning where he left off. My heart is not adequately shut, and I am starting to feel sick. That one thought, that we had so much to talk about, wants to drag me back to the belief that we had something, that he was something meant for me.

She's saying good-bye. She's hugging me. When I'm alone in the bathroom staring at my only slightly too-made-up reflection, I realize that I am newly hurt. His not being with Naomi is a fresh wound. His leaving me to go back to her obeys all the laws of nature. Any man would have done the same. But his leaving me just to be not with me aches all over again.

I find Martin mildly drunk at a little table talking to another gorgeous young woman. He motions for me to sit on his other side. "Come, there's room for both of you." Oh, brother.

"So Leo and Naomi aren't together?" I hear myself say.

"Shhhhhh. We're still marketing this thing. Shhhhhh," he says with Elmer Fudd eyes, glancing left, then right.

I need some air and maybe a cracker. A waiter passes with a tray of stuffed mushrooms and I put four on a napkin. I make my way to a terrace off the main room where people are still milling around but where there's room to breathe. I take a seat on the side of a fountain and dig in to my snack.

My parents have gone back to their hotel and they took Oscar with them, so I don't need to worry about the three of them. I guess I can leave anytime I want to. I need to unpack my feelings and then repack them more securely. But the air feels nice, crisp for Los Angeles I guess, and I am in the middle of my big moment. I wrote a movie and won an Oscar. I'm wearing this beautiful dress, and once I take it off, I don't know when I'll ever wear it again. I just want to sit and enjoy it a little longer.

"You okay?" It's Leo.

My mouth is full of mushrooms, so I cover it with my dirty napkin and mumble, "Sure."

"So congratulations, really," he says. "Okay if I sit down?"

"Thanks." I nod. He sits down right next to me, but not close enough that any of our parts are touching. My eyes track that space between us, as if it's something so familiar but from another lifetime.

"It's a big deal," he says.

"Yeah. For you too."

"Not really. I don't mean to seem jaded, but the first one felt like a bigger deal. And I can't get that excited about an award for acting like a total dick." He's flustered. "Oh, sorry."

"No offense taken, that's how I wrote it."

"Yeah. So are you happy? You said you were happy a while back."

"I am. My kids are good. I'm a big success." I look away, as if on the other side of me might be the answer, a better thing to say.

"Okay. That's what matters."

That's not what matters at all, I think. "That's not what matters at all," I say.

"Probably not. Sounded right though."

"Do you have a pencil?" I ask. He reaches into his coat pocket and hands me a pen. I can feel him watching me as I tie my hair in a knot and secure it with his pen. If only I could wash my face. I turn to him. "That's better."

He doesn't smile. Something hurts, and I'm glad. He says, "I guess I want you to know that what we had was the most important thing that's ever happened to me. And I'm glad it happened."

I hold his gaze as I consider this. It's a really nice thing to hear, but it sort of sounds like he's delivering the breakup speech he should have given me last spring. He wants to be let off the hook, and to my surprise, I find that I want to let him off the hook. I don't want him to feel bad about leaving me, and I sort of like the idea that he remembers it like I do. Maybe there are moments where people come together and you can just seal them in their own space while you move on with your life. Maybe what we had was a secret you keep hidden in a book to take out and ponder on your birthday. I smile at the thought because I know I've stolen it from a movie.

"What?" he asks.

"Nothing. I just hated *The Bridges of Madison County.*"

"The worst."

"All that pining away."

"And she saves that crappy linoleum table." We're both laughing, sort of. "I'm not going to hug you," he says.

"Okay."

"I just think it would be too much."

"What's this? The winners' circle?" Martin appears on the terrace with three young women.

Leo stands up to be introduced. The girls are talking in the most high-pitched voices I've ever heard, literally squealing with delight. Leo dons his gracious public persona as he talks to them. I'm still seated, dirty napkin in hand, and I ponder the fact that I've just been broken up with by a person I dated ten months ago. Was it gallant of him to address it, to acknowledge that it was actually something? Maybe. But did that balance out the thoughtlessness of leaving it unsaid for so long? If we were as close as I remember us being, if I didn't imagine the whole thing, he could have just said it. "I'm not coming back." I didn't anticipate that he'd turn out to be a coward, yet here we are.

I decide that I want to leave on this note. We've made a little peace; he probably doesn't feel guilty anymore. I got to hear that our thing was a thing. I'm in a gorgeous dress and

I'm about to make off with his pen. Let's roll the credits on this.

"I'm going to head out," I say to Martin. He grabs me and hugs me and says how happy he is for all of us. I'm to take his limo and have it return for him later.

I turn to Leo and the girls and say, as if they all have equal importance in my life, "Well, good night. Hope you all get home safely." And it feels like the second time I've won tonight.

I AM CERTAIN that if I can get back to my hotel, get into my pajamas, and wash my face raw, that all of life's mysteries will become perfectly clear to me. It's two A.M. by the time I'm out of the bathtub and in bed, Oscar on the pillow next to me, compliments of my parents.

Leo hasn't been with Naomi this whole time. He's been on his own or with dozens of other women who he decided are better than being with me. It wasn't like he was swept into some big love affair, he just left. I wasn't enough to come back for. At a minimum, I wasn't practical. I fall asleep clinging to new pieces of information: (1) Leo got drunk and told his family about me. (2) Leo isn't great to talk to; Leo's great at talking to me. (3) Our thing mattered to him.

I wake at ten o'clock because my kids are FaceTiming me. "You looked so pretty, Mommy. And I liked all the things you said." I don't remember anything I said, I'll have to look that up.

"Can I see the trophy?" Arthur asks and then laughs when

231

I show him Oscar tucked into bed next to me. He studies my face. "Did you talk to Leo?"

"Barely. He was sitting right in front of me, but there were a million people to talk to. Peter Harper is not as tall as you'd think."

Bernadette grabs the phone. "Ohmigod, Mom, Naomi looked so pretty. Could we do that with my hair?" There's a skirmish of some sort, Arthur wants her to shut up and give him the phone. I lie back on my pillow, relishing both the love I feel for these kids and the fact that I can hang up anytime I want.

"Want to hear something crazy?" I say. "Naomi and Leo were never even dating. It was all publicity for the movie." I'm not entirely sure why I feel the need to gossip with my kids. It's possible that I just need to say it to someone.

Bernadette's eyes go wide. "That's so sneaky. And it worked!"

Arthur seems hesitant. His face fills half the screen, and I think about how I can so often read his mind. He's running something through his processors; I can almost hear the *click click click* of it. Then again, one time I was sure he was being bullied at school, and it turned out he was just upset because I kept breaking the yokes on his egg sandwiches.

"Listen. Guys. Tell Penny I'll be there tonight; I'll come straight from the airport and maybe we can have a sleepover in her guest room—you guys, me, and Oscar."

They erupt in cheers before going back to their fight.

CHAPTER 23

I AM BACK IN LAUREL RIDGE FOR TWENTY-FOUR HOURS before the shit hits the fan. Looking back, I knew something was wrong with Arthur. I tried to tease his feelings out of him, but I didn't try hard enough. I was in so much pain for so long that I wasn't willing to make room for what was so obvious. There's nothing more shameful than this retrospective knowing, because it reminds you how blind you can be to things that don't jibe with the reality you're trying to believe in. It was the same way with Ben and Vicky Miller. I knew before I found the underwear. I probably knew what Ben was going to do before he did. I just didn't feel like knowing.

So when the school calls at noon and asks why Arthur's absent today, I know and I don't know. It's the Wednesday after the Oscars. I'd dropped them both in the traffic circle in front of school like any other day. I say as much to the attendance lady, and she is silent. I imagine this doesn't happen much at our school, which is why they're comfortable waiting until noon to call. I confess that I don't know where he is, but that I'll call her back.

I text him: Arthur? Text me back please. It's a full minute before he texts back: I'm fine Mom. I just need to do something. Don't be mad. Me: Where are you?

No reply.

I remember that I can track his phone. I curse my fumbling fingers as I try to remember how to log in. Finally, my phone finds him. He's in Harlem, and I go cold wondering what an eleven-year-old boy could be doing wandering around so far from home. I take a deep breath and pray to see with clearer eyes. I look again and see that he's on a train. It's moved already through 125th Street Station and is headed to the last stop, Grand Central Terminal.

It will take me ninety minutes to get to the city and anything can happen between now and then. I call Penny, and she doesn't answer. I call Leo.

"Hey."

"Arthur's missing," and I start to cry. "I need help."

Leo is clearheaded and decisive, where I am in a loud red fog. He tells me to drive to his apartment. He asks me for the log-in information so that he and Weezie can track Arthur's phone and get to where he is. I'm to go into his apartment and wait.

These things make sense. I say "thank you" a lot and head into the city. This doesn't feel like running away. What could he possibly need to do? Is he being bullied? Has he joined a gang and needs to follow through on some kind of a dare? Is this, at long last, something to do with porn?

I call Kate on the way and ask her to get Bernadette after school. I fill her in on what little I know and tell her to make something up to tell Bernadette. My adrenaline reserves are running thin and I'm out of ideas.

I picture Arthur sneaking off from the school playground and walking to the train station. I imagine him buying a ticket on the train because he wouldn't have a credit card to use at the kiosk. He would have chosen a two-seater and sat by the window, mustering up all of his courage for whatever it is he needs to do. It occurs to me that he's found Ben, that Ben's in New York and he's going to confront him. More than anything, I think about how little I've done to help him deal with his feelings, glossing over everything that's happened in the past two years. Self-correcting problem, my ass.

My phone beeps. It's Leo: Got him. See you at my apartment.

I cry the tears of a person who's lost everything and has had it casually handed back to her. Relief comes like actual waves and I find that I've slowed to forty miles per hour and people are passing me. I call Kate and cry until I'm over the Triborough Bridge.

I mop myself up as best I can, but I'm not overly concerned with my puffy eyes and red nose, a nose that I've been wiping on the sleeve of my peasant top for the past hour. Carole King with the flu. I am going to grab Arthur and smell his hair. I'm going to look deep into his beautiful eyes. And then I'm going to kill him.

The elevator opens, and I walk through the apartment

door without knocking. Arthur is on the couch next to Leo, they're watching *The Office*. Leo gives me a small smile, and Arthur looks like he knows he's in deep trouble.

"I'm sorry, Mom," he says as I sit down next to him and wrap him in my arms.

I hold his face in my hands and feel tears coming again. "Arthur, we can get through anything. Whatever it is, we can handle it together. I have a feeling there's a lot of pain we haven't sorted through, and that's my fault."

I feel Leo's eyes on me. "Where'd you find him?" I ask.

"The stinker was buying a donut in Grand Central, hiding in plain sight."

I laugh and hug Arthur again. "Well, thank you," to Leo. "My sister wasn't picking up and I didn't know who else to call."

"You should always call me." He turns off the TV and says to Arthur, "You ready to spill it? What's going on?"

Arthur stares at his hands. I touch his chin to try to get him to look at me, but he won't. I'm positive this is about porn. "Do you want to talk to me alone? Like without Leo here?" I ask.

"No," he says. "I came here to tell Leo anyway. You guys are going to hate me." Arthur seems terrified.

"I could never hate you," Leo says.

"I don't even think I'm allowed," I say.

Arthur takes a deep breath. "So, when Dad left, that was really shitty of him," he starts.

"Arthur," I say.

"Sorry, but it was."

"It was. Go on," I say.

"And you acted like it was no big deal, but it was a big deal to me. Because I don't have a dad anymore, like at all, but it also sucked that he could do that to you."

"It was shitty, I agree."

"So whenever I would think about him coming back, I'd end up imagining him finding us totally fine and like we didn't even need him. And he'd feel dumb. I think about that a lot. All of us just fine without him."

"Which we kind of are?" I ask. "I mean it sucks, but we have each other and Mimi and Papa. And our friends."

"Let him talk," Leo says. I take a deep breath and let Arthur go on.

"When Leo came, I thought how awesome it would be for Dad to show up and find Leo there instead. I liked to think of Dad driving up to our house and finding you and Leo on the porch, like all happy."

This stings. I can feel Leo watching me but I don't dare meet his eyes. "And that's how you'd get back at Dad?"

"I don't know. I just liked the idea that he'd leave again knowing we didn't want him. Yeah, I guess I'd be getting back at him."

"These feelings really make sense to me, sweetie. And I think daydreaming and talking about things is a good way to process anger. I just write and try to create a world I can control for a little while. But, wait, why did you come to the city?"

"To see Leo."

"Because you wanted to tell him this?"

"Because when he left us, everything hurt all over again. I

didn't care about the play that much, but just that he left like we didn't matter."

There's nothing I can do to conceal my hurt from Leo. My child is expressing the deepest part of my pain, thereby increasing it exponentially. Habit tells me to save face, to minimize the whole thing. But here's Arthur in pain, and it feels disrespectful to him to lie about mine.

"I felt like that too. Did you come here to tell him that? That's very brave."

"No. Here it is. The night of the play, Leo texted me to see how it was. And I killed it," he says to Leo. "I really was good. Anyway, I was mad that he left us, so I told him that Dad came back just as the curtain was going up, and that you two were back together and really happy."

I'm stunned. I'm staring at Arthur, who still has words coming out of his mouth. Leo is silent.

"I'm sorry," Arthur finishes.

"So this whole time? You thought Ben was back?" I say to Leo.

"I'm sorry," Arthur says again.

Leo is on his feet, hands on his head like he's trying to keep from hurting someone. "Is this a fucking joke?"

"I was mad at you." Arthur's voice is so small.

"Well, you broke my heart, dude," Leo says.

"Oh," is all I can manage. Everything's coming into place, the silence, the hostility. He really thought Ben was back. And the last piece: Leo's heart was broken too.

I take Arthur into my arms, because I know he's in a lot of pain. I feel a peace that surprises me, like when there's an explosion and then complete silence. That silence is a super silence, quieter than anything that came before. I know where Arthur is. I know what he's upset about. I didn't imagine this thing between Leo and me. He's not a monster.

"I was coming back," Leo is saying to Arthur, not me. "I don't know how I could have made that more clear. I know I left in a hurry, that's just kind of how my life is. Just because your dad's a dick doesn't mean I am. And you know what? Just because he hurt you doesn't mean you needed to hurt me." Leo's legitimately angry, and I tighten my grip on Arthur.

Arthur wiggles away from me and faces Leo. I feel like I'm not involved, like the two of them are working through their breakup, and I'm just there for moral support.

"Leo, I'm sorry. I think my mom loved you and I was trying to protect her. I shouldn't have lied." He's sitting up straight, looking Leo right in the eye. "And I owned up."

Leo stands there for a while, silent. "You did. But I feel like you just ran my whole life through a meat grinder." He starts walking toward the kitchen. "Maybe you guys should leave."

CHAPTER 24

I SORT OF FEEL BAD FOR ARTHUR BEING TRAPPED IN THE car with me for the ninety-minute drive home. I have a lot of mom things to say about his feelings and what happens when you misdirect your anger. We talk about the truth and how precious it is and about lies and how they can spread and take over your life. I have a lot to say about his dad that I probably should have said sooner.

"You know that your dad leaving had nothing to do with you, right?" I don't know how it's possible that it's taken me two years to say this.

"I could have been better at shortstop," he says to the window.

"You could have been Derek Jeter at shortstop and your dad would still have left. He loves you and Bernie, but he just doesn't know how to love his own life. You're good enough, Arthur. The problem is your dad doesn't think he is."

Arthur's looking out the window still, and I know I'm not being entirely honest. "When your dad and I were married, I kind of felt like you do. I thought that if I could do everything perfectly, we'd be happy."

"But you are perfect, Mom."

"Right?" I say, and we both laugh. "Love isn't something you need to earn. Dad left because of Dad, not us."

Arthur cries a little, says he's sorry a lot. I talk about the beauty of coming clean and giving and receiving forgiveness. It's a lot of talking, so much talking in fact that there is no room for the second set of thoughts that want to introduce themselves: Leo was coming back. Leo's heart was broken too. I tuck these away like I would a Wednesday crossword puzzle or a bag of chocolate pretzels. I will take them out and enjoy them when I am alone.

We pick up Bernadette at Kate's, and I promise to text her later with the details. We go home, we start homework, I make meatloaf. We read a chapter of the last *Harry Potter* book, and I insist everyone goes to their own bed.

When I've cleaned the kitchen and locked the doors, I pour myself a glass of wine. I feel as if I have to run the past ten months through a new lens. Leo thought I was back with Ben, that my kids had their family back. He thought Ben came back and my feelings turned on a dime. He even sent the money to make it look like he was a renter all those extra nights.

I hold my phone like it has a pulse. Leo should have texted by now: Wow that was crazy. Kids these days! Am I right? But no, he's really upset, and there's no text. Maybe just too much

242

time has passed. Maybe in that time he's fallen in love with someone else. That's hardly a stretch of the imagination.

I type a dozen texts and delete them. I feel like I should be apologizing, because Arthur is an offshoot of me. If I was a better mother, maybe he would have worked through all this anger by now. Maybe if I was a little less guarded, I wouldn't have let Leo walk away so easily. After all, I could have left a voicemail. If he'd known I was falling apart, he would have known it was all a lie.

I am startled by a text. Leo: Do you have something you want to say? I've seen text bubbles appear and disappear for the past 20 minutes.

Well, that's embarrassing. Me: I guess I don't really know what to say. I'm sorry this happened.

Leo: The whole thing?

Me: No just the end part

Leo: I'm leaving for New Zealand tomorrow for three months. Maybe we talk when I'm back

Me: Okay

And that's it. I hold my phone for a while to see if there's more, but there's not. It's okay, actually. I finish my wine and look at the black February night through the sunroom windows. The tea house is invisible tonight, but I know it's there.

IT'S MORNING, AND I'm feeling careful. There's a potential new reality out there, and I want to let it incubate. If I open my heart to it too fully, it will surely disappear. I have plenty of evidence to suggest that could happen. I decide not to tell my parents. I decide not to tell Penny. I decide that I'll just tuck it away like a fortune cookie that says, "Something nice might happen."

I will tend to Arthur and remember to check in on Bernadette to see if she's harboring that kind of hurt and anger. The thing about Bernadette is that she doesn't really harbor. She feels it, lets it out, and moves on. With Bernadette, the explosion usually happens in real time.

I creep downstairs and throw on my heaviest coat while the coffee brews. The February sunrise feels quicker somehow, like maybe the sun knows it doesn't have much time to get its work done.

I walk out onto the porch just as it's in midrise, and there on my swing is Leo. He's bundled up in a peacoat and a navy wool cap. He has a thermos and a hot mug of coffee. "Good morning," he says.

I sit next to him, unsure how close I'm supposed to be. "You must be freezing."

"I am."

"Aren't you supposed to be going to New Zealand?"

"I'm leaving in a little bit. I just thought maybe we could do this before I go."

He's looking at the sunrise, not me, so I follow suit. We watch as the remaining gray lightens to pink and then deep blue.

He turns to me. "So, this whole time you've been sitting here every morning by yourself."

"Yep."

"And every morning I was picturing you here with Ben. Ben in my spot, saying stupid stuff about things he'd never do. Ben putting you down. Ben in your bed. I was so angry."

"I thought you just ghosted me." I'm looking at my hands resting on my pajama bottoms, which are a bad flannel with too many colors. I fold the fabric to hide two mustard stains.

"Nora." He turns his whole body to me now, exasperated. "How was that a possibility given everything you know about me? That would have meant our whole thing was a lie."

I don't look at him. I'm afraid of what he'll see if he looks directly into my eyes. I nod. "That was the worst part. At some point I sort of figured I'd imagined it."

He turns back to the trees, and we're quiet for a while. There aren't a lot of birds, but there are a few hearty cardinals flying around, landing on leafless branches. Everything I wanted to say to Leo when we were apart doesn't make any sense anymore. All the story lines I'd devised to answer the question "Why?" are irrelevant.

And then it really hits me. "You seriously believed I'd just take Ben back? Were you even listening? Did you even watch the movie? Eew."

"I know. I've been wrestling with that all night. But I think when you love a ten-year-old kid and he tells you something, you just take it at face value. And you four were a family, if your kids could have had that back, I would never mess with that."

He takes my hand, just barely. He's touching the tips of

his fingers to mine, and we are both staring at them. It's nothing and everything, our hands touching. I say, "It was a crazy big lie."

"It was," he says. "And maybe the whole time I was here I felt like I was borrowing this. Like I didn't deserve to keep it."

"This?" I say, motioning to the rotting porch decking and the rusted chain on the swing.

"No, this," he says and squeezes my hand. He kisses me, and it's all back in a second—the dizzy swirly flood of happiness and excitement. It's last year again, and Leo's kissing me on the porch. Except it's not last year. It's this year, and I'm Me 2.0.

He pulls away but doesn't let go of my hand. "So I want to leave today and then come back. Like, here."

"Okay," I say. *Okay!* I mean.

"Like, I want you to know I'm coming back. And if you think I'm not coming back, then I want you to say, 'Hey, asshole, how come it seems like you're not coming back?' Like a normal woman."

I nod. "I should have said that. Would have saved a lot of trouble."

"We lost a lot of time. And it was horrible. No more of this stoic crap."

It's so nice to be sitting next to him on this swing that I'm doing a lot more feeling than listening. Leo wants me to know he's coming back. Leo's coming back. "Okay," I say.

"You know what? I don't trust you. Here." Leo grabs my left hand and shoves a thin gold band on my finger. This is less like a romantic gesture and more like the handcuffing of a fugitive. "We're married now, okay? Like in your head, just get that straight. This is happening."

I laugh because it's so absurd, and also because I am so light. A thousand pounds of hurt have been lifted off my chest. "Okay, we're married," I say, and he kisses me again. I can't help but think this is better than any wedding I could imagine.

"That's my mom's ring," he says. "It was the best I could do in the last three hours. But wear it till I get back, and then I'll get you a new big gross one if you want. To go with your marble countertops." He tilts his head to my new kitchen.

There's a car pulling into the driveway. Leo gives the driver a wave and makes no move to get up. "So you're coming back here? Like to live in Laurel Ridge?" I ask. Suddenly, the whole thing makes no sense.

"Sure. And everywhere else. We can figure it out. We're going to be together, wherever we need to be. I don't want any other life but that life."

Bernadette comes out to the porch and freezes when she sees Leo. "Your mom and I are getting married," he tells her.

She opens the kitchen door and screams into the house, "Arthur!"

Arthur comes out of the house already yelling at Bernadette to shut up when he sees the three of us snuggled up on the swing.

"Tell him," says Bernadette.

"We're getting married," says Leo.

"For real?" asks Arthur. I hold up my hand and show him the wedding ring.

He hugs Leo, then me, and I notice everyone's crying.

"Now go do your morning things. I've got to kiss your mom good-bye."

CHAPTER 25

I KNEW IT," MY DAD SAYS WHEN I'VE GOT THEM BOTH ON the phone. "The whole thing made no sense, and then we meet the guy and he's fawning over your mother like a fool."

My mother is crying. "He's just so handsome. I felt so badly for you. I looked straight into that young man's eyes and thought, 'Poor Nora's never going to get over this.'"

I call Penny and she makes me tell the story twice, which I enjoy because I'm still sort of telling myself the story. "You know what, you weren't ready for this relationship a year ago. Arthur did you a favor. Now he's back and you're ready." Ridiculous, but maybe.

"This whole time he thought you were with Ben," she says. "Gross. Thank God Arthur came clean about the whole thing. I see a wedding at Lake Como. That's where the Clooneys go. I can have Melissa's travel people look into it. Are you thinking fall? I'm thinking fall."

I look down at my little gold band. "Doesn't matter to me," I say.

I call Kate who conferences in Mickey at work. Mickey is swooning like maybe he's the bride here and hangs up so he can call Leo before his plane takes off.

I get a text from Luke. Hey. Welcome to the family. Jenn and I are so happy Leo's going to stop moping around. We'll celebrate when he gets back.

Weezie calls. "I'm speechless. Like he just called me and I cried the whole time. He says my first job is to get my shit together. So I'm trying." Weezie is already in New Zealand preparing for Leo's arrival. She's been given instructions to give his fiancée anything she asks for.

"You know I'm not going to ask for anything," I say.

"I know. And that's the best part." She's crying again.

IT'S MARCH AND the kids are on spring break. We are in New Zealand, on the set of *Ruin,* a romance Leo's starring in opposite Tatum Hunter, a younger, sweeter version of Naomi. I read the script on the plane and really couldn't get over all the sobbing and dead-eye staring into the distance. I guess this is what they'd call realistic romance. They don't do this on TRC. Their movies offer a sub-fantasy of resilience: The guy leaves and the girl is sad, but then thinks, *Hey, I still have my cupcakes and my friends and family. I'll be okay.* He returns to find her nearly thriving. He never returns to find her in the fetal position, clutching a fifth of gin.

Leo does the leaving in this movie, so Tatum does the sobbing. There are a few love scenes toward the beginning that, of course, we don't see filmed. Now the three of us are sitting up on a cliff, watching as they film Leo and Tatum walking on the beach. Arthur asks, "Is he going to have to kiss that girl?"

"Yes. Poor guy," I say and put my arm around him.

"Is that going to freak you out?" Bernadette asks. Bernadette, who's wearing sunglasses and a floppy hat like she doesn't want to be recognized, but really wants to be recognized.

"Nope. I don't think so. Well, I won't watch too closely."

A van pulls up behind us, and a man in our hotel's uniform asks, "Are you Mr. Vance's family?" He has a picnic lunch ready to be laid out.

"Yes," Arthur says before I can.

SOMEONE FROM THE *Post* gets their hands on a photo of the two of us watching the kids swim off the back of a boat in Milford Sound. The headline reads MEGA MARRIED. There's an insert where they've blown up a photo of my left hand to show Leo's mom's wedding ring, and the article goes on to speculate that we've had a secret wedding. Leo instructs his publicity people not to respond, because he likes the idea of it.

"First of all," he tells us over lunch by the hotel pool, "we are married. We got married on the porch. But this also means that we can have a wedding and no one's going to bug us. They think it already happened."

"Sneaky," says Arthur.

"Can we talk about the wedding? I have ideas," says Bernadette.

We're poolside but in a cabana that protects us both from the sun and curious passersby. It's available for us all day with sunscreen, snacks, and a bowl of orchids. Two uniformed men stand right outside to satisfy any thirst or whim that might come up. I'm in a bathing suit and my favorite white cover-up, but a box arrived this morning with several new, better cover-ups that were chosen by Weezie's stylist. They are beaded and fringed and sort of uncomfortable. I hope they are not a metaphor for this life I am entering.

I wonder if Ben knows about Leo and me. I wonder if he's at a location on the globe where people read the *Post*. How is it possible that I've ended up with the bigger life when I was always the one selling him the smaller things? I have a man who calls himself my butler waiting twenty inches away to refresh my iced tea, and I have to say that's pretty nice. But I don't want to end up at arm's distance from my life. I want to pick out my own bananas, watch the sunrise from my own porch.

"What do you think, Mom?" I've missed their whole wedding discussion.

"I think I want to marry Leo," I say.

Leo smiles at me. "Well, that's a relief. We're debating location."

Bernadette makes her case. "Let's rent out a castle in France. Like that big one where the Louis used to live. And everyone can stay there, and the wedding will be in the back garden. We'll make your hair high on your head like a queen."

My face shows my trepidation. "Was there another option?"

Leo says, "I say let's get married on the lawn in front of the tea house, with the door wide open so we can look out into the forest. Just family and our closest friends." He sees that Bernadette is rolling her eyes. "And Bernie gets full control over decorations. No budget."

Arthur says, "Can I pick the band?"

"Done."

My butler is removing my plate and is replacing it with a plate of the most exquisite fresh fruit I have ever seen. I can have this and a backyard wedding, I think. I wonder at the possibility of having it all.

CHAPTER 26

ᛒ

IN JULY, WE GET MARRIED. LEO AND BERNADETTE HAVE HIRED
a crew to create a canopy of white lights over the entire
back lawn. Leo and Arthur are in white linen suits. Bernadette and I wear simple white sundresses, chosen by Weezie.
It's hot, and at the last minute we all decide not to wear shoes.

There's no need to add color—the forest behind the tea
house is a curtain of all shades of green. Above it is a clear
summer sky. On either side of the tea house's open door is the
annual explosion of blue hydrangea. They welcome me down
the aisle, perfectly framing Leo in my line of sight. Leo's here
in July. And he's staying for all of the Julys after this. Something blue, indeed.

After the ceremony, we move to the front yard, which has
been transformed by candlelit tables, a band, and a dance
floor. The caterers have taken over my kitchen and my porch,

but the whole place still feels like home. The trees that sur-
round the property give a feeling of privacy that I never really
felt like I needed before. Laurel Ridge might be the perfect
place for a celebrity to get married.

Luke gets up to make a toast about how I turned his
brother into a real person. Leo rolls his eyes and gives me a
squeeze. "Mom was so proud of you. She tried not to brag
about you, but she couldn't help herself," he goes on. "And
this family you've wiggled your way into, this is what she
would have bragged about the most." Leo takes my hand and
kisses it.

There's something extraordinarily celebratory about this
wedding. It's not just because the people there love us and
want us to be happy. It might be because they lived through
the time that we were apart and miserable. It might be because
they all either lived through or saw the movie version of my
marriage to Ben. Luke and Jenn, Kate and Mickey. Even Mr.
Mapleton seems profoundly relieved that Leo turned out to be
a good guy. Penny and Rick make Leo promise that we'll come
to their annual white party in East Hampton. Mr. and Mrs.
Sasaki spend the whole night on the dance floor.

Weezie is giddy. "I met Nora right here last year," she tells
my parents. "She was worried we'd wreck her lawn, and she
was right. And all the while there's this thing brewing between her and Leo."

Martin is there with Candy, who appears to be back in the
rotation. "I take full responsibility for this," he tells everybody. "It was my idea to film here. I brought Leo right to her
door and let him sleep on her lawn."

·   ·   ·

I AM FALLING asleep in my bed with Leo, because he's my husband now and that's legit. We're lying as close as we would be if we were still in the daybed in the tea house. I have two thoughts that I can't shake. First, that dance floor is going to wreck my lawn for the summer. And second, that the best things come back. Sometimes it's right after the commercial, sometimes it takes longer. But time and sunshine bring growth, and life unfolds just the way it's supposed to.

My husband whispers in my ear. "You still awake?"

"Yes," I say, though I'm nodding off.

"There's a part for Arthur in a film I'm thinking about doing in the fall. He'd play my son."

"Where?"

"England."

Nothing's how I planned, and I'm speeding into a future I can't quite visualize. Life imitating art, imitating life, imitating art. "Let's talk about this over the sunrise tomorrow," I say.

ACKNOWLEDGMENTS

In her impromptu acceptance speech, Nora says that she's grateful that her story was welcomed and nurtured by such talented people. I know just how she feels. A heart full of thanks to my agent Marly Rusoff for her immediate and enduring enthusiasm for this book. I could not be in more able or more caring hands. Working with editor Tara Singh Carlson has been a flat-out thrill. Thank you, Tara, for shining your laser focus on this book and for being so kind every step of the way. Thank you to Sally Kim for giving me the opportunity to share this book with the world, and to everyone at G. P. Putnam's Sons for making it happen, particularly the very patient Ashley Di Dio.

Thank you to my dear writing friends, who told me this book had legs in its very early stages—Lynda Cohen Loigman, Karen Dukess, and Steve Lewis. Without you it would still be a one-hundred-page Word document and a twinkle in my eye. I'll say it for the millionth time—there is nothing that embodies the spirit of generosity more than writers who make time for other writers' work.

A particular thank-you to my mostly adult children, Dain, Tommy, and Quinn, who read an early draft of this book under duress and for money. Your notes, honesty, and interest in the process were actually my favorite parts of this project. And Tom, the leading man in my favorite love story, thank you for your quiet faith in me and for reading it for free.